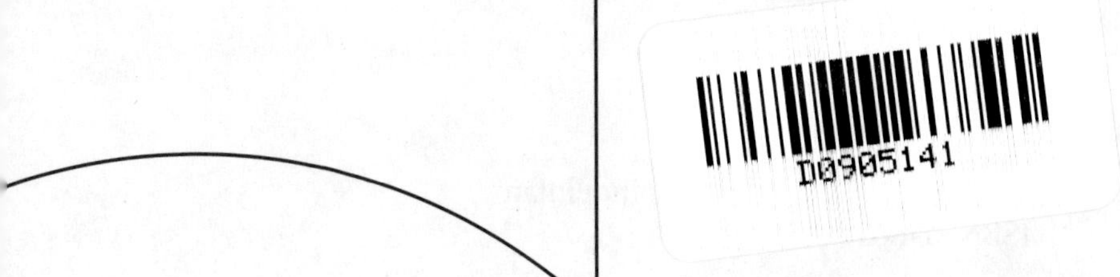

ARC: *CLEAVAGE OF GHOSTS*

a novel by Noam Mor

cover design by Margot Spindelman
ISBN 1-881471-79-9

Spuyten Duyvil
PO Box 1852
Cathedral Station
NYC 10025
http://spuytenduyvil.net
1-800-886-5304

Library of Congress Cataloging-in-Publication Data

Mor, Noam.
The cleavage of ghosts / Noam Mor.
p. cm. Arc ; bk. 1
Cabala -- Fiction. Mysticism -- Fiction.
Occult fiction. gsafd Jewish fiction. lcsh
12504934

Printed in Canada

Cleavage of Ghosts

The Argument

The Main character, Adam, nicknamed Stone, has three names, Aiulah, Atman and Kadman. Aiulah/Atman is the primordial person and Kadman is the transformed individual of the Kabbalah. Other Kabbalistic characters are Sheckanah, the primordial mother, and Shuckles Crown Mollusk, akin to spiritual wisdom. As many of the characters are parts of a larger mystical whole, Adam is merely a disunited whole trying to understand and integrate these into his person. His transformation, to be understood by the reader, requires that you aid in his construction, each reading forming Adam anew.

Phoenix

Cocytus

1.

Forgive me—You say—I am not your Phoenix anymore—I let the lack line sink then reel it through the dense river, petroleum-streaked banks exposed around my toes, like corrupted flesh, sticking onto your navel, pubic hair and bone. I watch your asymmetrical eyes float above the waterline.

Is anything alive even near?—Is the only thing you repeat while I fish—Anything alive even near? N'one can see me this way you know.

Like when you decided to skinny-dip and almost got jumped?

N'one's safe anymore. I'm lucky I'm quick—You caterwaul then move toward shore.

You're lucky they were slow—Sitting on my calves compressing my thighs I imagine a line halving you through your breastplate.

N'one gets me.

Some sparrows frantically fly in untrue circles. Huddled by the river, our toes numb in our hands, a clarinet bellows your laughter with each gulp of air.

Not even you.

Disturbed we flee to the warmth of our rented skiff, blanket covered and wine. A flugelhorn crashes as I kiss your moistness, regard your closeness, a french horn belching notes rocking a slow march through the first snow of my loins.

Downstream, a collie is heard jumping after a midget on his tricycle, riding at differing speeds on the steep riverbank in order to test his physicality. In the center of this river, I anxiously hear your sounds, waiting for your whim of a box that hides.

The midget rolls from the bank, his head just below the demarcation line marked on our stick to find out if this river is ebbing, is saved by his collie. The stone you always had, purple, covered in pin pricks, you file over my back, eating me and being quick about it; gnashing my teeth, I say—From this day I will be with you indefinitely—This man-fed river rushes down to its berth full of cans, marijuana seeds, krill and our skiff(in anticipation of rocking and sunlight, my eyes transfixed on peeled paint behind you)I feel vibrations and a sudden lurch against my prow.

I gladly make love to you—You say—I am yours, don't you know?—Playing with my bulb of urethra—Do you see?—and—Are you mine?—
In fear of your blood running down my legs and my slowing hip, I am unable to answer, pressing your buttocks tightly between my fingers. You smile, I imagine, because in my closed eyes I act out this lie. Crouched like a dog sniffing, I follow each rib and smell you, like the Sargasso Sea, intwining Kali.

You are mine—I say, you echoing—I refrain.

2.

The Midget, his head still engulfed, tries to find his way without abandoning the tricycle, his dog dry heaving from too much saving. On the skiff, I look away from your gaze.

I need to find something larger—You repeat, holding my element within your fist—I need to latch on to somebody more enviable than me. I am tired of the poor—Until I have the strength to deny your milk, I tacitly agree(I have no fear of unspoken lies)Your saliva drips on me.

I don't know how long you mold me into a pod that, taken from between your toes and tied to a string is allowed to float and grow while you sleep, into the Earth. Beyond your shoulder, seeing the lilacs of your pillow, I bite the back of your neck like a mating iguana trying to pacify, only this time I pinch your jugular and enter and take your blood, your white cells clamping onto me like the seams of a scar, haphazardly swelling and shrinking. Holding my stone to your ear, you hear, I am told, the sea.

It's beautiful so early. I only hear the river.

I woke up with the sun.

It's tremendous to see it rise. I ought to do it more often.

Tomorrow then?—I ask, hearing your deletion.

Yes, tomorrow I will get up for the sunrise. If tomorrow comes and I arise.

Today I rise late looking for you, getting dressed with havoc to rush out to the bench, yesterday's written date, a still half empty bottle of beer and the river an inch lower than our line.

I didn't want to bother you.

Today is a red day?—I refer to your nails.

Today is a red day because the bees are not out and I don't have to worry about my allergies or work. And I have decided based on my knowledge of you—You say, adding a link.

We found animals, once a dying dog unable to lift its head; with time and caring we brought it back. At first, its head rose only a drop, cracked tongue licking chomps and trying to wag its tail; one day it even smiled, a half snarl, you know how dogs smile. Then we placed the food further, forcing it to stand, agonizingly close taking one or two steps, staring at us until I finally broke down and nudged the food. Soon it rose when I entered the room wagging its tail furious—Pulling your head, your hair frizzy and dry smelling of newly cut hay to my thigh—It existed to give me pleasure, to piss and to eat; just to be with or without passion. For me. It was obedient to me; that simple. I loved that dog. I look for its submissive passion. Where is your submissive passion?—You excoriate.

3.

The American Anthem plays as the station closes, waking me to your empty chair; the coffee covered by film and stagnant in the middle of my room illuminated beneath the lamp on my night table with lion feet. The clock radio bursts two hands flat slapping a keyboard till I am reminded of your I need things while drinking gin from a mug, letting your tongue hang on its rim. Yes—I repeat—Yes—my abdomen recoiling at your suggestion of my subsumption.

Yes—out in one breath—I need someone who'll own things even if that means giving themselves up for me—Eyeballs hiding in my skull crawl out to investigate you grabbing your breast and finishing my drink.

Only a big fat tit to you.

Waiting, drawing out this last statement—Or more of your accumulating dust?—You leer(just like a dog laughs)and I flick my hand.

Urgently, back on shore the Midget follows an orbit whose diameter increases, irregardless of his collie's wrangling or one sparrow and another until an entire extended family becomes hoarse, or the water growing deeper. He yells across to me.

You, held against the Saguaro, why aren't you dead or at least fatally stabbed?

Fading behind the trees, the Midget and his collie leave, his physicality displayed in his inability to continue on as long as my thoughts go on. This is what we are I believe. Watching the Hot Bagel sign, you rise, surrounding the cigarette with your lips and playing a glance to me. Stroking the mug, you drop both, the cigarette twisting beneath your boot tip and the glass shattering—I don't want you here—and—Remember to leave the keys. It's

preset—
You jump into the water, your crimson bath suit splintering the sun behind my eyes; laughing, hair wet, you swim to the other side and, as always, bring me to you. I imagine, submerged and hanging between your legs, hearing the door slam, you turning left following a widening ripple. You don't bring me to shore; I am floundering.

You Without Arms

Leaning against the prow, I sit on burlap, my heels pressed against your seat, legs surrounding my memory of you drinking Budweiser, your immobility, cheeks taut like stretched fine grain hide(your painstaking deciphering abating)looking at the boat's bottom, measuring the slow leak's progress.

The skiff's leaking, ya' know.

Yea, we'll just have to get to shore quicker.

You hope ardently for a large change in overall depth. With another sip, I am still dry as the sky becomes orange.

In bright red, you walk by, torso rocking with the burden of no arms; beginning to skip, you halt, aware of my watching.

Do you have no arms? What are you?

Slowly skipping away between the trees, you zigzag to escape.

Do you have no arms? What are you?

Your spike heels tear the grass as you run from me.

Can you touch me, Phoenix?

Your feet tangle, sending you sprawling into a tree, slithering against its bark.

Let me hold you, Phoenix. Come hear.

Your eyes are almost completely egg white, pupils tiny; you spit toward me, letting your mouth uncharacteristically hang and pant.

Phoenix. Please let me touch you.

Rushing over the bridge your torso twisting as if about to tear(I am ecstatic because you are exhausted; I sense your vulnerability your
franticness)Pushing harder to arrest you, I dribble and see you hide in the abandoned carousel beyond heavy weeds. I scatter the cats, sending them to the river, a yellow-jacket circling. I see you slithering through the bars, pushing them aside with your left cheekbone, inadvertently licking rust.

Phoenix, hold me again. Why won't you stay with me?

Climbing into the carousel, I find you indolently seated on a carriage led by earless horses.

Leave me alone or I'll give you syphilis—You say tiredly. Almost tearing your lily print dress I don't recognize my fingers, arthritically twisted and unable to hold, the joints bloated. Unable to sustain the pain, I let go, wandering again.

Bringing the skiff to shore, I scratch the earth, sounds other than the traffic and two cats crying like hysterical infants. I can feel its moistness burying my feet. Branches cut my calves and tangle my hair before I reach the oldest tree I reclaim, gnarled with many cysts, horizontally folded receding into the ground, its roots and stunted limbs allowing a dry spot and faint moonlight and garbage truck sounds to permeate. Having refound this place, I want(in your thin cotton nightgown decorated with red postmen)to invite you to my hole; reliving my revenge, I hope you see what rains on your porch and is smeared on your door.

One Piece at a Time

Peeling white paint uncovers streaks of cooler lime green. I inhale rapidly, smothering my half-finished cigarette just to light another while caressing my chest hairs. Drawing one out to its full length, I try to pull it out but stop. A mahogany brown cockroach escapes along a crack beginning on the ceiling, running from the toilet. On the northeast side, the crack extends in a crooked line southeasterly into a cigarette-sized hole through the floor. Sitting on the damp seat hoping to find you today. I've already begun excusing you.

I cannot swallow my saliva like a rank fish tank or remain leaning against the orange flowered wall, surprised my senses aren't reeling. Slapping my clothes, I find an ash spot; trying to remove it with spit, my fingers roil madly through small mats and tangles of hair. I want to look well before my pocket mirror reflecting one piece of me each time; an eye a nose and a loose tangle of hair or(in front of the full-length mirror a surprise)standing shorter than you although you were not taller, just much firmer, inviolate when you decided. After another drag, I desecrate you with a uniform.

I stand for a smoke outside my pink cylindrical building, my room seventy two inches round, a steeple across from the yellow church(I have never heard its bell ring)At this point of Vaudeville street I can see the duck pond and

Copulation in the park, chrome cylinders forming half a cracked walnut surrounding a black metal pentameter torn and warped like a woman crouching, her two arms reaching outside the perimeters of her shell, but unable to touch the base or a single sheet beyond her like a chador lying dirtied.
Receding blue green and red reflection soaks into the pond like mud, reaching the cliffs on its south side. Clearly closer than I know is safe.

Is it safe this close?

Heh?—He is solicitous

Is it safe this close!

Why no but can't you hear the Siren's song?

No, you'll have to take the cotton from my ears—
Still immovable he says—Why can't you?

I'm tied up, as you can see—Obligingly he says—
O'yes. Just a minute.
He removes the cotton gauze.

Epistle—The Stains

Landlady says with pride, her back to me, in mock confidence

> The house has withstood all these years, the snow, the rain, the blizzards of sixty seven and sixty eight. It is haunted by a woman who cleaned everything with thick ammonia till her septum disintegrated. And all her senses.

Clutching my arm to imprint each word, she reiterates

> All her senses. Near the end, she walked up and down these steps, all thirteen steps fifty times each day, never more nor less, stopping at the bottom to think, through the hallway door, on the street. She

would touch the knob and turn and pull, unable to budge it 'cause I keep it well locked. This lady would look past the iron gate and wire-reinforced glass.

Pointing hectically to these images, still holding me

Her name was Phoenix. Her eyes were very red and her lips were black, that's right black, pointed down into points, like this...

Landlady, beginning at the center of her upper lip, moves her fingers down right and left past the lower lip, then stops

As if she painted sad each morning. You were always able to see each wrinkle on her face, then, after watching for all different number of times, her brain just burning till you could smell it, she went back never looking back. I saw this, so I know.

Landlady, beating into her chest, becomes quieter, letting go of me

Never shut her apartment for fear, I guess, of not being able to get out. This lady was homely, a woman who wore thick mascara and multi-colored blush each shade.

Her hands, colored like a turkey's wattle, rise to her eyes

Darker as it approached her eyes. I am much prettier than she ever was.

Landlady says, pirouetting then groaning as she slowly reaches to pick up her dropped key

They were emerald green, her eyes, and were like slow ice, you know, always moving even when she didn't bataneye. Can you imagine? Painting her sadness in the mornings?

She stops here, shaking her head heavily, this her only pity for a woman she thinks of clearly and can never not speak of. I close my eyes from her and the thick air like algaestill water. Closing the door, landlady leaves me in your room of cadmium yellow; you often said

I can't think and look at this color simultaneously, a place I can hide in the dark while my eyes are still open.

Foam from your torn red pillows and a scant pile of seeds litter the wooden floor. On the wall St. Luke is scribbled

Launch out into the deep and let down your nets for a draught.

A reply scrawled two inches below

Cockroaches, only Amphibian Cockroaches are found here.

In an attempt to erase these stains, the dialogue continues

I must find roots.

Roots almost touching the floor right above an inferior rendering of the Tree of Life, with what seems to be your face and on the floor is scratched

Kri.

Unattainable and saturating, I imagine you leisurely smile, older, your hands twisted like damaged wings rushing through your small print Bible. Hearing an ambulance go past, clattering against the wall till its sounds reach into the corner near the radiator spewing steam, dissipating. Curled in the dark of my armpit, sniffing occasionally to remain aware of where I am, my legs fold to my chin reaching further into my skull.

Grabbing The Snake with my fingers, I toss it deeper into Cocytus(in some places He must be there but He I don't see or touch or smell or taste even when full of the most overpowering expurgations)I cannot intuit He.

On the street, Landlady jumps on her motorcycle, pumping against the starter with thin ankles, her clouds of breath dense like the engine resounding. Recklessly she rushes to the locksmith almost hitting a youth carrying a giant radio and letting each step fall two half beats long. He has all the time in this world riding on his youth and Landlady on her age. And I am middle age, even now too gone.

I'm—

Touching myself, I feel the pain from a pinch of my genitals as I rock my masculinity against the living room rug, only feeling friction and remembering your hold on mine.

I feel wonderful feeling orgasm through Man
I feel wonderful feeling orgasm through
I feel wonderful feeling orgasm—Phoenix said.

Buddha tried to become negation, trying not to be, becoming heaven. Perhaps I can stop my intensity. But I speak hearsay.

Her dentures removed, Mother wrote—Through His son's sacrifice, we are of Him and enter heaven with Him, which is the Son which is Him which is the Holy Ghost which is All—Always capitalizing Him, Son and Holy Ghost, writing—I had you because of an unpredictable menstrual cycle—I think she is mad, having written unintelligible things. Having left the house to escape her words(in vain)

Snowing, the flakes push against the pains, covering the gutters and the steps, it too quiet for this empty room.

Does Landlady know it is so cold?

Does she know I am cold?

Does He know I am here? It can't be bothered with, I don't know He. I speak hearsay again. I waste my time speaking of heresy again.

She's doing it! The old whore, she's locking me in! Just turning the cylinder, that simple act disturbing my reverie and sealing my fate and now I can't get out. Maybe she'll let me out in a little while, a month or so. I wonder

how long.
That Priest, a youngish man who played Ringolivio told me the holy ghost is phenomenological spirit and I have it. I went to strangers with this news.

Do you have the holy ghost 'cause I do!

Yelled from my diagram to strangers till they gave me pennies for tootsie rolls and to stop my begging. The Priest said,

The holy ghost is spirit!

Damn it! I've done it again. She's heard me, I can already hear her scrapping along the kitchen floor, preparing to search. I wonder if she knows of me? Knows of here? I wish my masculinity would stop thudding, not at all the thing I felt with you. You were thin and rare with your chiffon blouses and thick black lips. I wish you weren't here and this stain wasn't here. Ala-Kazam! And everything we have isn't; I'm I ask and I ask is it enough to just keep repeating like a recording machine questions of self? Will it adhere to the I?
My God, she's walking up the steps, she's coming to let me out. But where will I go? Damn, she's rattled up these steps, opened the lock and peeked; telling me to leave, asking what I'm still here for and beginning to swear about the stain. I wonder where I'll go? That's the best thing, just to have a drink to decide after rushing past her. Damn, I better close my pants.

Expurgations

My favorite stripper, her tag spelled CAT, wearing a palm-leaf leotard emphasizing the tensility of her breasts, comes after my drink. Rising, I say—Don't wander off as I may(or all of me)end losing ourselves to necessity in

this brothel—Beginning toward the men's room, my eyes slide across CAT opening and becoming lost, stinging a sore on my tongue. CAT's sandpaper lips succulently drape a morsel and
another.
I watched you, pudgy and worn pale, rollicking in black leather and a new red hat, meeting another for coffee by the river we alone shared. You said, lamenting on our six square feet of sand, what you and I could become in our dissipating time, why you could not see me if I didn't—Why do you row me into this morass? Like a tumor, you sit on me—Chewing, you turned away, walking down a dim street in high heels, uncomfortably pursued one empty lot and two empty lot blocks to there(The Midget urinated on a nearby bush three times, perhaps trying to smother it, each time glancing at you to be sure you recognized an association or possibly noting your watching and aversion)Searching for a link in Sunday's rehearsed chain but only able to repeat(changed through its generations)your watching through a windshield my urination, headlights shining onto my opaque masculinity like gray clay on your porch(I wanted you to awe; face me repeatedly spurned)To denote territory or to spit at someone from a distance.

An insult worse than a slap on my face, because it is as if liquid excrement were poured on me to denote I am owned.

It's time to go to the river—Kissing only the air you were intent on castrating me in passionless repetitions.

CAT, a tight pink bow accentuating her throat, brings another drink—Want another private showing, Stone?—Her long red nails tapping time on my chest with a wail. Behind the black walls, watching her undress meticulously, expressly against my will but not my wish. I say to the woman next to me—Excuse me, but do you have a light?—She does, a sudden bass voice.

Do you come here often?

Yes.

Is it perpetually this empty?

What does perpetually mean? But it should pick up and the music climb a few decibels, if that's what you mean. Good music like the Apoplectics. I've seen you here before.

Yes, but I don't remember you.

Do you dance?

Not really, with men.

I'm a little shocked. No? Oh, what a shame. You're cute. How did you know? Do you want a drink?—I hesitate but he assesses, interrupting—Yes, you have come here before—Feedback fills the silence of a few people rubbing their hands through beige hair or wigs, waiting.

No, I can't admit I've thought about it—Trying to hurry along, stopping, hearing his predilection for men—Buy me lots of drinks and maybe I'll let you, if I might—Hoping this will disgust him, used as supplier, but he is so cocksure—I will have you later—He assumes while finishing his drink—Yes I will. Here, take another drink and I'll return in a moment. Yes, I'm sure you come here often and are just coy. Got to go to the ladies room, you know—A clarinet breathless gasps six times, his giggles swish amongst the tables.

Alright, where is it?—Eve says to Adam.

It's gotta be here somewhere.

If you've got it—She coos—It'll have to be below the navel; that's where to look. Can we conquer this thing?

Sure, after all, it works for the lower animals.

No, wait, yes, I'm crazy about you. I don't want anything to do with you; your acorn sized rod can go home and...

Looking at him she stops, realizing.

Hell, you've got your choice of cock—Drawing closer, he begins—I would love to lick you from head to toe.

Drink—She responds remarkably unperturbed—We're predetermined; I will know you for nine hundred and thirty years—Taking him between thumb and fore-finger—I wish I had a broader selection, but you're the only cock in town as far as I know, Adam.

On the last sip of my rusty nail, they are not there. I think of your leer.

Alright—Assessing him, tempted to pretend—Hey, Bartender, give this Zweigeschlechtliche Menschheit, Androgenous Mankind, another drink—Raising his glass, he winks just before he drinks.

CAT dances beneath the strobe light. I want to take his lips, lead him to the dance floor and, while he strokes my back, I want to know you are here tonight, how you felt unfastening your safety pin as we heard Bolero.

Do you wanna come?

He lies on his blue blanket tattered at the ends covering orange azaleas on a backdrop of discolored white, boots touching headboard, concentrating on his fluctuating light bulb, shadows spackling the mud colored floor.

Here I am—He says, pulling his legs down to opposite ends and rubbing his tongue across his painted lips.

You're almost here, legs outlined beneath translucent silk; a veil dropped before his sex; your eyes closed and your fingers crushing, ascending.

Do you want me to take you with your clothes on, Shy Boy?—fleeing down the warped wood steps painted charcoal, the neon night sign announcing Midwestern Fried Chicken.

Teresias

A woman with CAT's legs sits on a cushioned chair to my left, legs thrown over its arm, letting her negligee fall below her shade. I cannot see nor hear her smoking a thin blunt in the dim light emphasizing the smoke and her hazy shadow, through a cat mask with whiskers. The Snake wraps itself around my groin methodically compressing six swings(my chronometer set at full measure)She banging her gold and silver plated ring similarly, runs her index finger from her right knee into her shadow while I drink the vodka replaced within my pocket, its neck still visible. The Snake's pronged tongue flickers my solar plexus the breath in me drawn out after another swig and my throat drying. She who plays CAT unsnaps my pants. The Snake lies calm on my left collar bone its muscles vibrating a coiled line from my groin.

Just the right size for a pig roast—She laughs CAT's laugh. The Snake fondles my larynx never blinking its eyes. She says in CAT's voice—How is it feeling?

I feel like fifty heads and a hundred hands and heavy as iron.

Turn over so I can spank your gluttonous maximus—The Snake finds my eye sockets.

Open your eyes.

I am searching.

You don't need to search while I'm holding your Tree of Life.

I feel like Teresias—The Snake investigates my grinning skull.

Just start at the Tree of Knowledge and point it in the right direction.

The Snake curls into a ball within my cranium.

Now it's in the right place, Mr. Teresias—with CAT's laugh.

Latin alto voices rise to frail children repeating fifteen syllables, their voices fading with Hermaphrodite's dismantling. A silver plastic barbut with plastic ivory horn tapering upward circles in the air, her torso swinging in half moons twice each group of fifteen syllables hesitating as the chanters breathe(her breasts never sway)her thighs pulsating. She places the wedding shawl upon her left shoulder, straightening her torso and tightening her bicep, first touching the horn and her left hand reclining on her iliac crest(her striated belly passes me, her pubic shining beneath the vaseline)when the bells overcry the children she turns barbut facing me—Good evening, Dear Teresias, glad you could come—Falling heavily onto her palms she pulls her body prone; trapezoids and breasts(dugs squat and caramel)expanding and failing—Why Salve Festa Dies—She says cariously smiling. Unsnapping my pants and entering me.

First Teacher

Phoenix, where are you?—We are in the middle of the pond and you are swimming easterly—Don't go! You know I can't swim!

Running on my toes like a sprinter caught on a treadmill an unknown distance below me, inhaling colloidal dust and dirt, the algae-thick surface soaking up air and

blocking out sun. Mouth closed, my fingers fall below my eyes fixated down to find an image of the sediment. Unable to smell my hole of sienna I am like a child calling for his mother while the water like wet canvas binds around me head to toe drying and constricting(fixated upwards, I see glimmerings and attempt to decipher the surface, my outstretched arms always reaching to the largest still perceivable glimmer dissipating)my cheeks breath bulbously then concavely. I hear a bark, a parakeets' whistling and an approaching; am wrapped very tightly in drying canvas to prevent all chances of escape, to prevent my webbed hands and feet paddling away.
To guarantee we'll stay together.
Close, he is familiar, but only his outline reaches through my canvas gauze.

What is your name?

we're floating, tightly bound. You know my appearances well because you see me each day. I never pass you but am always with you

I recognize your voice. You are the midget trying to drown yourself

we're drowning and continuing to drown

that's impossible, I can hear you, however vaguely, sucking in air

sucking water. We are sucking in the pond, what else would you say we're experiencing

only the last thing I remember tells me I'm drowning, but I can't be speaking and drowning at the same time

you aren't speaking

who are you and why don't you help me?

I'm Stone, that's why I'm here

I'm Stone, that's why I don't help you.

The Snake splashes, dropping from a nearby willow tree,

partially coiled it seems as long as an Anaconda I imagine twenty feet and long enough to kill Man. The Snake begins swimming toward me, tongue flickering to find me by heat and flailing to stay alive as long as I can.

Phoenix don't leave me! You know I can't swim! The Snake swims closer, sensing dying, your fingers reach between my toes suckled and bitten, The Snake's mandibularian muscles contract, searching for an anchor to begin climbing, licking my achilles tendon your fingers clasp around my calves beginning an indian burn. Winding upward The Snake squeezes my tendons forcing one knee to bend ending my kicking, you bite the back of my knee gently holding my tendons with your mandibles until my leg reclines against your navel and breast. The Snake surrounds my thighs climbing toward my abdominal wall, you lick my thigh nails walking my urethra. The Snake's head buries itself into my scrotum tongue flickering in the marginally warmer wrinkled skin. Toying with Man's masculinity you use it as a stepping stone, washing over me and my glans quivering; I let The Snake take me falling back to escape the inevitable tide coming in.

I know I'm dying
and I am
free of the canvas blanket. One red spermatozoa, its tail whipping, moves through a brown and gray rain of changing depth toward blue tails disappearing into a just born whirlpool. Darkness is the water I breath.

Boxes

1.

Fishing, I smack the catch into my prow.

Why'd you do that?

`Cause I have the ability to watch you die—I draw closer to watch my success, now safely in the bucket, she says,

Hey Stone, no water seems to be coming from those concrete pipes anymore, did you know?

No, I've only measured its fall on that stick close to shore. Do they pump sewage into the river?

It's only a puddle and they call it Cocytus.

Cocytus? Isn't that a much larger sort of mostly uncharted place?

The municipality built this extension.

Have you ever been to a mostly uncharted place?

I can't be sure, since I'm not sure if those—Beginning to aspire—places weren't this muddy—Her gills inhale large amounts of water rapidly—overflow. Anyway, I remember being lost some amount of time, as now, but there being so much space and so many things chasing me. Anyway, I'm not sure that was, here nor there. I can only say I, until just recently, was an employee of this town.

What was your job?

My job was to be fished. Simply stated, to be caught. It's the Human Services Branch, but they've negated my employment—Taking a pause approximately as long as the time to read these words, she continues—And thereby me. The municipality says I never occurred.

Are you sure?

They don't have it written on any municipality lists and their records show a building's here.

But we're standing on part of it, looking at part of it, hearing parts of it. Smell this, just smell this soil.
A soil covered pebble drops, sinking, but she moves aside.

All I know is they claim a building's here and I'm cracked. They claim my whole story isn't verifiable.

What's their address? I'll find the records of your story.

You can't; they're closed.

Damn, but I can almost touch you!
Leaning on her side, rubbing her belly against the bottom, Ms. Catfish continues.

It's unimportant. I'm in a dream in my final conversation on somebody else's line.
She lays against the bottom, her pectoral fins fluttering slowly.

You're beginning to look pale. Are you alright?

Of course not, this bucket's kind'a small and that sadistic smack on my head—Her tail angling higher than her head—But what did you say about those five senses? Perhaps there are six, some sort of intuition? Didn't you think of taking that into account?

I'm not sure what I'm getting at.

Haven't you dreamt and once awoken thought it had actually taken place?

Rarely, and only after the deepest sleep.

Haven't you ever believed what was done wasn't possible?

I'm suspect.

Couldn't this be that impossible frame? Couldn't this be that...
Her pectoral fins move once then remain motionless.

time?

You're dealing with noncorporeals and they're intangible.

Doesn't all, especially those most deeply rooted things, have to be processed by the mind?

Yes.

Are the mind's processes tangible or intangible?

I don't know what I'm getting at.

Can Idontknowwhat be definitively corporeal? If something is perceived by an amorphous process, can we be sure of its corporeality?

Slumping, her gills inhale once more, her tail angling further.

I guess not, Ms...What's your name? Why are you dying?

We're wonderful; we're fine. I'm a phoenix that came back as a fish. Another mistake. Anyway, let's get back to it. Can we be sure anything was, being as we must always use an intangible process?

Why do you always say was rather than is?

Her gills exhale, turning belly up she rolls.

Under an elm tree, the snow cold underneath me, I try to read the paper about an altercation at the Parks Department between a woman(name withheld upon the request of her parents who avoid acknowledging her profession, saying she is always lost)and a Parks Department employee who explains she `...isn't on our employment lists...' categorically stating `...her position just doesn't exist, therefore, your six month claimed employment history is invalid and such checks included...' At this point, the article states, the police arrived, but the woman still cannot be found.

But I remember her gestures, tones, her lips and the way she inhaled the scent of my penis.

2.

I rise from the grass spackled with snow, a squat caramel church surrounded(each wall barb wire tipped)a castle-chinked roof and an arched doorway casting a preceding shadow, glossy red tiled crosses embedded in the stone to the right of its oaken doors the only passion color. A black cat slithers through the cast iron gate of black spirals chained shut. Pint bottles litter the square; I touch mine for comfort. Perhaps I was thrown over, as were the other bottles, reminding the hermetical priest of a world that will not begin. Entering the confessional box, Father opens his windowless darkness.

Father I fear I have done wrong—That is why I wait—Perhaps I have killed a woman?—Perhaps? We can not seek absolution for sins you are not sure have been committed. Who?—Shifting his buttocks.

I think I've killed Phoenix.

The bird that rises again?

She keeps rising from the dead in my dreams.

God is telling you something. Do you mean a person or the bird?

My lover.

Did you kill her or only want her dead?

I'm not sure, but I think I killed her as a fish. There were times I wish she were dead.

Do you think you killed your lover in a dream? I'm not sure this is a sin.

What is there in sin?
Trying to smell the darkness.

God gave us his image and he is pure good. He gave us his law to follow and obey eternally. God gave us souls—Souls assume we survive past the grave. Just like Phoenix returning as a fish—Reincarnation is not the answer to your riddle. You will have to look into your soul. He must mean something with this fish-phoenix-thing—It was a catfish. Do they have souls?—God is omnipotent, omniscient, the creator, eternal. He created catfish. They must have something—If God gives catfishes souls and it had Pheonix's voice, then I might have wanted her to die. This is the sin I have committed. I've desired someone's death. And then she died.

I intuit confusion from the void.

It is immoral to want someone to die. God can forgive your heart.

Why do I need his forgiveness? If God knows I'm going to commit evil and doesn't stop me, doesn't God commit sin also?—God can't commit sin; we do not know the ways of the lord. We can not grasp his direction since he already knows all. You should go home and relax. Why have you come here? You aren't willing to have faith, to understand it.

How can I relax if I wanted Phoenix dead!

I hear the Father's window close, imagine him kissing his holy shawl.

That's it, I came here to find faith! Father, why can't you tell me where it is? I cannot forget you through your silence.

Only in this darkness of a confessional am I forced to doubt, in the darkness am I forced to break my silence and confront it.

Why did she appear as a fish? Why did I ram her with my prow?

I poke at my masculinity, wondering if I should take hold of it, pressing against the seams of my pants. I call to Phoenix through the curtain.

3.

On the shoreline's brown grass men indefinitely act, one his hair braided and flat, having one eye painted above his nose and another on his tattooed chest, circles in loin cloth around a kneeling-man while another man in leopard skin on a raised high back throne mouths words to his counterpart repeating

I'm the world and there's no escape nor doorway even above.

His counterpart beats the ground with a large ivory staff carved in repeating identical rectangles while the one-eyed-man, his cheeks riddled, grasps the center of his horn, varied sacks ruddled at its tapered tip and spins, stopping before the kneeling-man canting to the enthroned-man. The kneeling man tries to beg without lips as the one-eyed-man rushes about him arms and beads flagellating

Marked in red ocher
Sacrificial blood of Earth
Marked in red ocher
Tonight you will go West

Throwing a large sack from the horn into the kneeling-man's eyes

We must tie him to a tree
And a fire begun
And the heretic's bones
Cleansed

Before the kneeling-man, the one-eyed-man begins violently undulating his hip as if he has a woman raising his cudgel

Disclaimed
the hundredth name
The hundredth tongue

Three jackals with
Three heads
Shall devour—

Tonight—Says the enthroned-man—We are eating well—But a motley-man skips from invisible to visible

We
Begotten and Buried
In the same blink
Of an eye...

He cannot finish due to laughter from the enthroned-man rising, also beating his cudgel into the kneeling-man, repeating

I'm the world and there's no escape nor doorway even above.

Resurfacing

I am surprised how fluent I am in this pond, my bulk sleek and buoyant, more powerful than I expected. Wiping away some water clouding my vision, I see the surface is surrounded by white polished plastic. Sanitary, I wait but can't catch sight of any air bubbles rising. While balanced on my toes, reflected in the mirror, I finally have enough fear to open my eyes. Pitifully I can't retreat to the features I see or recognize these. I hope I am almost born rather than just dead.

Miming

Redressing, I chose my black underwear and pants, my black shirt and jacket and my black faceless watch.
I want to feel hollow in these.
Down three sets of nine steps, five then nine through a corridor with one centered silver stripe on the left wall to a room that is dark, a breeze coming from the west a little too cool for me. A wail weaves tasseled and black, like dull red and a little yellow rocking. I search for a switch, only highlighting a few chairs and tables within a few inches of the door, no exit seen, only more chairs and tables imprinted with checkerboards and backgammonboards fading into the predominant darkness, placed to form two vertical aisles north(I am at the south wall)and another perpendicular aisle going either west or east or neither. On a checkerboard are chess pieces strewn across and, sure of nothing else to do, I begin preparing for a game, the breeze as soon as I begin increasing and declining when I am finished, at which point The Midget comes from the horizontal aisle and, posited on my chair, asks what color I will be.

White, as I was here first and am accustomed to playing with white.

Don't you hear the music? I've been here as long as you, waiting to begin—A throb of voice rises and becomes sedate in much the same way as the breeze.

Then white because I prepared the pieces.

But—He says—You misunderstand. We are spontaneous.

Let's just flip a coin—After which

White it's heads for you, Stone.

Pawn to Queen Four; King's Knight to Bishop Three;

Pawn to King Three; Pawn to Queen's Knight Three.
I offer The Midget some of my drink, but he only says,

Aren't we losing? You can only build a fortress so high till crumbling begins. That's from the Tower of Babble and it is absurd to believe this game pursues a victor.

We can't both be losing. Games are designed to have victors.

One's cancellation will lead to the other's.

Pawn to Queen's Rook Four; Knight to Rook Three; Bishop to King Two; Castling.

Games are designed to have victors—I repeat as an axiom.

Rising from his chair, he paces the wooden floor another time

I hear a voice, that voice, where does it come from?

Didn't you come in with whoever it is?

I thought you came from it?

No, no, our people are gone. I go out and come in with you. Don't you realize we came in together?

Even your whole game is miming me.

That's right. It has no choice.

Pawn to King's Rook Four; Pawn to Knight Three; Queen to Queen three.
He walks beyond our lighted circle

Where are you going? Are you leaving? I can't see you—The Midget moves back into darkness.

I'm going to find a door. I'm at a wall. There isn't a door, just some scribbling on the wall.

What does it say?

The room is rectangular. Babble! I can't make out what it's saying—Back in my seat he says—Perhaps there's a window.

Bishop to Knight Two: King to Knight Two; Rook to Rook One.

Did you find any apertures?

I couldn't find apertures of any sort, it's so dark. This circle we play in is the only light—Bobbing my right knee on my left knee while I try to think of the game before me, wondering if there is a way to extricate myself from our miming but it leads to parallel repetitions, one move requiring another identical move toward a goal I don't have any inkling. So I begin to kill.

Queen to Queen One; Knight to Knight Five; Bishop Nixes Knight; Bishop Nixes Rook Pawn; Rook Nixes Bishop.

I've found a window—He says

But where?

In your musings. Come and see but watch your step, it's very dark.

Damn, why won't this window open!—We heave on either side thinking of breaking the glass and scanning the darkness for an object.

Queen Nixes Rook; Queen Nixes Queen.

I have you now, Midget, I have your queen and there is nothing for your next repetition—Remember, we are simultaneous—Where did you put mine?—We come and we must leave together.

The glass is shattered and neither of us bleeding. Lost in darkness, feeling bars just beyond the sill, I search for a padlock. I wonder where The Midget has gone.

What did it say?

What?—I hear The Midget from somewhere in the darkness, I believe in the direction of the breeze.

The scribblings.

Oh, a picture, vaguely like an ark with one sail, I guess, and a roof above it, to block out the sun.

Anything else?

Some letters, 'HI...', and two other worn letters I can't make out. Unfinished. It used to mean something.

It still does, but is it the same?

I leave the game to refind the window. Feeling with my hands, I look for another passageway, or the original doorway, moving toward the still too cool breeze, directionless, looking for the wall scribblings.

INSOMNIA

1.

Staring hard into the darkness for some time now(This place has no breadth nor width nor length which can be seen)I can't arrive nowhere or anywhere. This determines my unhinging; slowly, haphazardly, neithersoutheast-northnorwest(I can't decipher the direction I'm following)How can it be if it isn't of these four? Up; perhaps down? I feel neither compression nor hollowness; even falling, I have felt these.
I must recall reconstruct and recapitulate to escape from this unlit hole(has it occurred naturally or accidentally?)I recall trying to sleep but the smelling excrement, it is distributed upon the tile, and sharp urea...sharply. What did I do before now?
A brief reconstructed moment, a chain of moments, a mute, a chain of mutes, a day...or even longer. My documentation should be here, within my pockets. It should all be here.
A lot of scribbled notes
A credit card (I touch the embossed characters of my name)
some change
An empty bottle
A pocket watch which ticks
A course of action
A course of belief

A lot of conversation
A really intangible method...
Where is it? My social security card isn't here. Sharp and unevenly cut edges. 620651455, memory of a place before this, but it's not here. Only the urine smell. God it's thick, making even sight impossible(not even shadows are here)Is my mortality here? Is that it? Taken so another can claim me, this number beginning new debris, gaining my birthdate, passage to an identity while I'm locked up here. But am I in a prison? My head pounds, listening to the thicket of my watch. Have I been replaced, am I expunged? I cannot recollect or imagine the next step or the last. I can only estimate I may have died undecided, without time to negotiate my sins(I look for a crowd of rope to hang with, but I have never found one)Here! Here! Here is a second memory)My hand, I think, is held before me(it isn't seen)exhaling and inhaling rapidly and shallowly.
It can rub our faces.

Is this a grave? Is this a night?

I wave my hands before my eyes and look for a moon. A boundary again, another limitation.
There is no moon
there is no light or not enough light to see(could I be blind?)
the sound of a conch(could it be water?)
it is becoming hotter
no rope or glass(or I haven't found either)
I cannot see the direction I go.
I must piece together my condition to bridge my time.
I only remember my lost card(will I ever have it?)
it is warm(but the past, let me lead to it)
I don't know my master here(is there a god here?)
I am not able to tell the difference between the flies,

crickets or cicadae(even the insects are ambiguous here)they will not show themselves.
Man, I sit by my visions, constructing my scent when burned
sulphur and carbon, I wear perfumes to cover this odor
yet I am odorous
I am colorless
my meat is not tender
I have many sounds and shapes
        Where is my card?
I am Man.
62045 1455
620 45 1455
A cataract pouring me down.
But what is in this plunge?
        Enough! Be rid of this place!
        These things
        Uncover my internal hiding!
        Stop this noise!
        Uncover this grave!
        Enough!

2.

Enough!—Is that an echo or another?
Its roots lead way down into the earth, reaching the core(our birth)and above it are branches full of faces and before it is an effeminate body, whose weight rests on its right leg the color of veins. A child looks out from its branches, staring at the amber light of an eclipse, holy and yet sparkling.

Who said enough? Who is here! I have a right to know my surroundings!
Leaning against mortar chipping and cold, searching the quiet.
Could it be me, could I be here?
Quiet but for the breathing of a conch(it waits)perhaps I am dead. Whenever we are unsure, we could be, unless there is something sure to begin from. Not knowing what I want and feeling too weak to bother creating or destroying, so I let other things and doings draw on without me. A slug lying on the floor, I will have to begin and move. My fingers crawl over my face, insects rushing by my lips, breath and abdominal organs tightening. A tile floor, the smell of urea, stone walls and the sounds of water dripping(I must be in some bathroom)

I will not believe
I will not believe this
I will not believe this place
I will not believe this place is
I will not believe this place is a urinal.

I doubt; therefore I am, at least if I assume thinking(but this does not help me escape my thoughts)It seems a correct step, but do I only exist in my doubts? Is doubting enough? I am better off waiting for the morning, if it comes(even the sun is impermanent)to tell me the way.

But this place may not let in light. Lead.
I am led each day to my choices and my beliefs by media and talk and the confluence and continuation of patterns and activities(what choices have I made?)There is little else to do here but decide. I must choose to continue or to curl up
and burn in my salt.
I recall Phoenix's legs drawn to her chest, tight and about to hit the water, our buttocks touching on the bed. Her closeness disturbs my insularity now. I am suddenly awake, expelling and contracting, trying to force her up(I want to regurgitate soon but will not be able to)I delve deeper into my arms. Eventually I will have no place to go and will try to slither further(further?)Underground? Let me try and pinch myself yes, I feel it, and the motion of redistributing my buttocks on the tile. If I could find the card beside me, it would be
a first crumb.

3.

Time to arise. Time to get up. Time to search.
Let me hear again.
My forefinger inches along the wall as a scout, slips over a sharpness. Beating my right fist into it, I bleed(glad to be suckling and tasting my own mortality)In my head, I can see nothing but an uncertainty. My patterns adhere, like embedded cysts and must be burned out.
I imagine holding onto a stainless steel bar as another(my arm solidly wedged in place)applies the red hot iron cube. Burning, my teeth bite hard into the gauze, to create scars(scars are necessary if we are to survive)to become
men(I need a(women.
The fire shivers through my arm. Men in loin cloths dance; others, fat breasted, walk to me by the fire, prodding as they would tease an outsider(a boy)Dancers swing their hips more wildly, their hands reaching down and holding air(Old men's tits hang, they are remembering)With gray steam, the ejaculation of
seamen(cleansed from all the old materials)da dudumdu du du du duda dudumdum du du dudumd du da dudumd da
We drip.
It rains(I am unsure)recognizing foottaps.
Who is here with me? Answer me!
Some life is enjoying my fear(if it is a panther and can smell it?)Laughable! Ridiculous! A panther can't speak...In death? Is this what death is like? To be in total darkness, smelling urea and shit? Maybe I am not dead(I really do not want to be dead)but someplace. All I can remember is trying to find someplace, but what place have I found? God, this urine is distracting. Many men

must pee here. Where do many men pee?(Is it even human piss? Couldn't it be dogs or apes)Or Woman? I am not a connoisseur. The animals and men all do it on the streets now; I've seen it many times. This could be the streets. But if I were on the streets I would feel a breeze or hear some hum of some sort, or something. There is only the tapping of the rain(maybe not the rain)I would see(not if I'm blind)If I heard a voice, I cannot possibly be dead. My logic is so dying, a desperate man who doesn't want to be dead. How can I know if death is not voices? Perhaps death is eternal voices. If I found the card, would it assure me I'm alive? My logic is such a dying man.

Please, God, let me hear your voice again.

Perhaps, if I am silent, the enough will be the answer. I shall, I know it I know it, recognize it again.

Why must I search for you!

Oh, I have a headache now, there isn't any point in asking questions of a thing which won't answer. I have to continue on. Perhaps I'll find greener pastures. Yes, and perhaps I'll find a wild boar. I haven't seen where I am. Maybe that's why I'm here, I've been told the truth time after time and refused to believe it and so they put me here. Who are they? A they or he would explain so much qualm and doubt. I've always believed I was they or him, but just because I am or think or might be dead I weaken. I must be strong; I remember thinking even upon death I should not weaken in my beliefs. I don't want to believe in an external They or He(no, not even a She)I've continued because, in the end, I've counted on my belief there is some permanent truth. I've always just assumed there was some unchanging truth. Perhaps this is death, a questioning of whether it is immutable or whether truth isn't something that changes from one day to the next. A circumstantial thing? The floor is covered in some sticky film(our filth)

Please, please tell me who or what has said enough—I am so weak, as if I were traveling and have landed and feel jet lag and lost—Just tell me if you have my social security card? If you're beginning in my name?

I respond because you beg.

My breathing slows, I try to recall. Even now, several seconds after, I wonder who it could be. Could it be me? Could I have begun speaking to myself without registering that it was me?

Who are you?—Already, my voice hollow and weak. I want to see him.

For a newcomer, you ask too much. I have been here as long as you. You've woken me up.

Where are you? You must have it!—Waving my hands erratically, I begin searching in my immediate vicinity.

Don't be so dense. I don't need it and, besides how could you accuse someone you don't know? Don't bother to search the area; I can see you, but you may never see me.

Who are you, that I may never see you?—Stretching my arm back so I know he isn't behind, I have gone too far to touch the wall.

I am Kadman. Who are you?

Just Adam.

If you must move around, please do so quietly. I want to fall back asleep—Kadman says—All your answers are not in this place.

What do you know of my uncertainty?

You constantly fondle your genitals, isn't that enough?

Enough? Enough for what?

The lady doth protest too much.

What, if anything, do you know?

I've overheard.

Heard what?

Your lack of faith; your inability to be certain, even about being alive—What have I said? Could I have told a secret in my sleep? Was I asleep?

There you go, your genitals touched again.

My hands hover across the floor for an artifact of recognition.

How are you able to see me and I not you?

Hidden away as another. First, you should know what thing can be absolute.

Truth?

Truth changes with the process that finds it. No, truth is a dangerous way.

Is there another way?

Begin with me, something less than a solid.

To begin with you, I must know where who you are.

I'm contagious.

I sweep my hands in the direction of Kadman's laughter.

Show yourself! Show yourself with the insects, Father of Insects, Father of Man. Kadman!

What's matter?

wait.

Better left to decomposing.

4.

I can still stand, what a relief. Not to stand is like impotence. I've often thought of suicide if I couldn't stand. I will have to crawl to find the card(I pee in Kadman's direction, hoping to splash him)Without a foreground or horizon, I am dizzy, moving my hand across the broken tile, my only orientation the wall like a shoreline.
I wonder what superstitions I should be careful of here?

Kadman, is there escape?

Go to sleep.

Did you take my card?

Go to sleep—Kadman says as if for the last time.

What's your full name, Kadman?—Remaining unanswered, I trace the outline of a crack, leading to its closure, a textual mark in the dark.

SOMNABULISTS

1.

Do you have Visionary dreams? Do you sometimes sleep and then awaken in another place and know that this is really a place that tells what there is in the world when you are awake?—Kadman speaks from ahead.

This is the prize before me, my thinking, my pushing and murmuring. Putting my hands against my horizon, I feel feverish in the thick heat, wondering if I can remember and relieve an episode of my life(beginning with a fragment of my back entering, walking in, repeated three four five times)A doorless doorway. But I wait that I might turn at the last minute.

Beginning my reckonings, I force myself to attempt an invention(simultaneously I interfere with my meanderings, not wishing to believe what I see, turning aside and not continuing, finding another event)each leading back to an unfinished series. Is this my atonement? To remember and relive through my mirror exchanged glances between my reflection and my watching? I look to my watch to see the hours I have been here, but the watch no longer ticks and I cannot see it's face to know when it stopped. I start to repeat the numbers of my card(but they help me no further)Remembering to count, trying to trace a crawling path beyond the blankness with my eyes. I take another step to find a door to any other place. My darkness and this darkness are confluent, the sound

thick with flies, crickets, cicadae, the ground with silverfish one hundred segments long. Footsteps crawl fast upward from my hand(toward my ear)but I swivel and kick from the darkness we are in. I would follow any activity to avoid this tangle of thought(there is no food, no television, no radio, no electricity in my discoveries)I am filthy and there seems to be no way to wash. Will I get lice, fleas and ticks(my abdoman's panging)Is this my impalement? That's it, I will do pushups and situps, the escape of movement(even of these I can do perhaps nineteen and thirty five, it cannot last long)The momentary sweetness of my muscle pain, then I will fall backward again, back to the ground into the scum, idoling.
I wipe an itch on my scalp, predicting my future so easily. Curling up with the pain of self bereavement(suckling my thumb, I let all my front teeth hold it)I can bite this. Ones, twos, threes, fours, fives, sixes, sevens, eights, nines(bending my last fingers)tens. I beat my chest, wishing to be solid as a rock, an idol, massive(but my stomach cramps)I have not concentrated on my breathing(I need to concentrate on my breathing)With all the illusions of these circumstances, I harden and am subsumed by my blood. Eventually, a chance of illusions.

I have more endurance
I have more endurance than(like stone)
I have more endurance than I hold
I have more endurance than I realize...No

Not as much as continents.
I struggle to incarcerate these things. Recollect these things. It is re-evaluating our innards, each piece, a recapitulation, a number of mediations beyond this; going back to remember the rain, it hastens on, ignoring our uncertainty.
I find myself in a strange foreign land.

Beyond an intuition that is a glimpse of yesterday.
I shall rise from my youth(finally back to it)I will grow from this place, my written words(in the muck of the tile, '620651455' scrawled, incomplete in its inception)As with certain religious people, thoughts becoming reactions. If not, I fail. Each thought and action a translation of gods.

Yes—Kadman says.

I am so lost, that is why I've begun to collect shards of memory. That's why I'm searching for my card.

It'll start a history, your parts and ourselves. At least you'll have found something. 620...the father...65...the mother...1455...us. A knowledge of self instead of things.

What do you mean?

It is necessary, but not the only place to begin.
I wait for the courage to scourge these temptations(a Medusa, snakes slither upon my head)Entanglements(I scramble at my scalp)
Recite a nursery rhyme, just to hear my name.

Adam and Eve went up the hill

Adam and Eve met a stranger, asking who she was

...Heaven's own child

The Tempest wild...She replied.

To find the place I want to lie in, my dreaming becoming too full of confusion. But this does not help(my eyes follow me)
Somnambulists.

It is all the same.

Even to this rendering.

It is all the same.

2.

Is my soul this darkness?

The black haze doesn't seep, disallowing images.

Bastard! Who am I here! Father of insects!—

Again, I receive no response.

Kadman? Kadman, are you there?

I'm still here.

Won't you tell me where at least?

I don't know how to tell you.

3.

Knowing this pyramid like a native(its space has become my blanket)I look upward for its apex and go further, drawn to my recombining(my scattering)to Kadman and the rain. It is so dark and the moon must be behind the roof(in order to keep things comprehensible I rely on this roof because, otherwise, would I be on earth?)I must design an escape route(we are always escaping)

I'm afraid of you, Adam.

What do you mean?

Of your wantonness, then your impotence, or first your impotence then your wantonness, or of any singular attack.

You can't be afraid of me. We've never met.

I've known you an inestimable time. Why do you think you hide?

I need sleep, Adam—I say.

We are things of the past traveling only to the past. Of course, we could transform with each consideration of our times and beliefs—Kadman continues.

I watch, won't close my eyes, try to find an organism in the darkness, but the image of others is vague and intrudes; only my hand holding and releasing with each passing breath, knowing I am still here and still alive.

You want to find me? There is the incommunicable between us—Kadman says—Here is a first principle, the incommunicable.

What kind? Can it be crossed?

This is your soul.

I sit and hug myself. Close my eyes—Maybe we should go to my boudoir of pink lace curtains and fuck me again. I was there all night waiting and perhaps it isn't like all the others, as I said, but longer, if that is what

makes you so uneasy. Perhaps we should tumble from the bed to the floor, A little excitement perhaps?—Phoenix entices, encircles, disperses me. I begin to feel nothing else, so I concentrate on her and our undulations, to become mesmerized by my groin—When I write, I think of fucking you. When I dream, I remember to fuck you. When I create, I can not but think of fucking you. When I sit and read and disagree, I think of fucking you. My energy of thought is intertwined with fucking you—I escape for a second into her place, but its insulation does not carry far nor last long—I don't want to need to fuck you anymore!—Trying to burn her out—Look at me Son—Mother says, pointing to her abdomen—Just touch me here where babies live and grow—I cautiously touch it—Of this—Sephira, the mother, repeats—And more—Her voice dissipating in the distance of my dream(she sits with squatters around a mound, their fingers running over it, shaped into something
thing
indiscriminately human)having left me
and I had not been able to touch our
distended belly.
This is the beginning of my deconstruction.

Awake! You're flailing alive!

Mother! Will this drown me? Mother?

Just another slow Australian crawl—Kadman responds from ahead, but the destiny of our air again becomes too thick to swim through(I hold on to my lifesaver)searching for him.

Mother! Oh, Mother, when will the air calm? Will I drown in my air?
Her wings envelope me like a small mouse beneath an eagle(screaming I am caught in these talons)

DON'T! PLEASE DON'T!! NOT JUST NOW!!

Will you let me go to sleep!
Knuckling my eyes awake, the pain of my gash reminding me of my skin. I try to find my ambient energy, to sit and be worn and show perfect indifference to my fate and Kadman's criticism, but Kadman is my only other here.
Walking another foot(the fifth or sixth measured foot)separated from the rest(I cannot be sure without clear sight)searching for a hint
of horizon, how many inches I will have to go. Beyond my boundaries it is still too dark to see.
This is why I flail.

Kadman, I do not want to think about where you could be or what or who. I want to know. Give me some direction, south east north or west.

It won't help. You haven't been able to hold straight. This is why I withhold information.

So I can make a straight line, so I could know who you are?

If I just go ahead and tell you, you'll forget eventually.

Your power?

What? You've changed the subject; I lost it some time ago. It is a passion. You seem to desire the loss of your passions. This is why you are weak.

No, their control.

It is the same for you, loss or control

but power has produced

(the repetitions in which is to be found energy that is necessary and extinguishing)

repetition of work
of fornication
of prodigy
of custom
from generation to generation

not to jeopardize yourself for a stranger and all are strangers

not to disbelieve in gods

God

or the godliness of Man

The morning prayers

in yourself

to have progeny

the repetition of our fear of bodily pain

and

And Yes

the repetition and unrecognition of risking the soul

the repetitions of our hiding thoughts.

Can I reach into a straight line?

I look for my place here. This is the secret to rebirth, a stoking of madness(it's emergence)feeding no one and only wishing to feed itself.

It takes my energy and leaves

me weak(like the moss of semen during masturbation)I must find enough strength.

Will I have enough time?

I can find no way to stop, because to stop would leave me nothing but to wonder why I had stopped(wondering why I go)I try not to consider the why, because this effort consumes me, will be a presence until my dying(the stop and the why are already)It is the doing.

What did you reel in as my soul?

The numbers in the card are our ghosts— Kadman answers.

Impunity. For protection, a defensive prose, positionless, but I have succumbed(I tried to find if I could be a sort of buddha, but I have succumbed)I am fallen like a too weakstick in everything. A twig I lack we, a place to forget the passing of my time, a place.

I am getting hungry, Kadman. Is there anything to eat here?

Wait.

I'm hungry, Kadman!

You've lain here too long to starve.

What can I do?

Leave me. Go to Hell!—He laughs with this. I slump in my hole glimpsing my wrists.

How long? How long shall I wait for the manna?

4.

Scuttling across the floor in ameboid shapes, not circles or straight lines, hooking for the card and other memories to construct an existence I can have. My rewatching moulds different scenes(provoked three dimensionally as another reality)to occupy my space and time. I salivate(gliding my tongue along my cartaceous teeth)at my vision of a young Balthus girl, before a lotus print screen, her skirt drawn uncovering her right thigh, a young prepubescent thigh. Half asleep, she rolls her eyes(I find rolled eyes tantalizing)

Are you a Balthus girl?—I say to Kadman, but receive no reply. I unsnap my pants and imagine my right thigh, fondling my genitals behind a newly found pillar(too large a circumference to wrap my arms around to imagine it a lover)Adoring my flesh to diversion is the first cardinal sin, Man's narcissism(needing to be secure at all costs)at all costs we ascribe ourselves importance. I conceive of the need for someone to tell me I am important, so that I might perceive importance. For otherwise I am nought. My shirt lifted(my abdomen's shivering)I slap my belly hard, to clean the bacteria within me, from my days' old clothes stained, rubbing fervently until I am scarred, finishing another indian burn.

This pain does not clean my house.

What bacteria floats within you?

This is all I can think about.

Think of where the rain comes from.

It doesn't have to come from any place—I say, thinking afterwards. Dwindling here before these cracks, trying to catch sight of my lacking, but all I see is a different quality of darkness without a definite image, a wall. Using it as my protector, a border, a pastime difficult to escape and to stop.

Having faith.

When does one have faith, Kadman?

After a long pause, the brick back in its place—I do not know if you do not.

You just said I didn't.

I just like to tease.

Is faith good to have?

Necessary and dangerously misleading.

Kadman, did you steal my card?

We've always had it.

What do you mean, we?

Kadman spits.

Understand, or you'll have to get used to it here—Accustomed? Could one, even for a second, become used to this, make this an even livable place? I press my hands against the tile, trying to dig to a discovery, but my knuckles pound. Crouching, I press my knuckles into a kiss. I must believe there is no more than one corner, only to believe there is no other place(if I multiply them, their danger can increase)I wonder if I will even find Kadman and our places.

You will not find some object to dig with.

A prayer from the past, trying to reconstruct, prying farther and then a little more for my lineage, my father and mother; she I remember discontinuously rushing around the house ordering us to go so she could clean and the arriving home of father hours later with comic books. For many years these things went on becoming the ritual of our tribe. I must decide to stop or die or go further into the ambiguity, past the borderlines I have made(my constantly relocated borderline)to enter this funiculus or retreat, I am very tired—Just let me whisper the directions to you—I lean toward me—It will come to you. No one can hear us anymore, they are too busy and too far away—I believe till I can extend my forefingers no further, that we will go on to another shore, but we are confused and then I am gone and the darkness is returned.

We must go further with impunity, with indifference—Kadman repeats.

I touch my twisting abdomen and leave—Tell me some gossip about yourself. I never slept with someone I know nothing about—A woman said.

And this time?

It was just something hot and stimulating to pass the time.

I will eventually be famous—I said.

For what?

For getting into you.

But what if it hadn't come to pass?

It is not hard to believe and will be remembered as truth for rumors are quicker, more digestible than truth.

Tell me some gossip about yourself. I've never slept with someone I know nothing about.

Truth is that thing we must understand with thought and emotion simultaneously. That is our only truth, It is not learned without—Kadman reminds.

I don't understand
It is not learned without
it is not of religion
not of blind faith
it is beyond these things
this place.

Will I find it?—I have not received a reply and recant—Kadman, tell me I am important. Irreplaceable. Kadman! Why have you stopped answering me. Shaman! God, where are you?

I attempt the opposites of habit, of personal traditions(this will be my whip)escapes from habituation. Rising from my buttocks, shifting darkness, moist mornings. I touch my thinning hair, hair of a weak man, applying spit to hide(we do not so easily hide ourselves)Smearing the moistness across my face.

I don't love, others do—Kadman yells from ahead so I might better understand. Trying to forgo myself(so much that I am disguised)I hear my sounds without recognition, feel the smoothness of my forearm, take a long inhalation without a cigarette, touch my skin again and hallucinate the odors of burning rice and tobacco. Grinding my teeth against the cold, not recalling where I have found(I cannot remember where I was just before this)sweat retreats into my right eye and burns. I touch my nose again, arm kept extended outward, moving perpendicular with my body, elbow bent. I only hear crickets' wings other than myself breathing(I cannot hear Kadman breathe though I listen intently)I imagine a desolation of sounds(encircling me with its song)feel empty of my history, isolated from viewing the past and discovering all potential futures, a now like the waving white silk sheets I see with my eyes closed; opaque and telling nothing.

I throw a bottle to hear it shatter.

Why can't I sleep this away? Where can I go?

Don't you have a place to go?—Kadman almost beseeches.

I am like you; I've found no place to go.

We cannot stay here.

We cannot stay and we don't know where to go.

Speak for yourself—Kadman distances himself.

I want to be golden again, malleable, charismatic and rare—I say, looking for another's flesh but finding

none.
Drawing a line, I open my eyes(a possibility)and find each breath shallow and heavy, blinking hard to see better than I have been made to see, recognizing this pyramid perhaps is not as vast as my delusions. What frightens me now is the shrinking(from an unknown space to what could be a coffin)Between them is where the potential lies. Each time I think of the past, it is chatter, another occurrence, subtly different then before, aged crippled and searching for catharsis.

Oh God, please give me the tapping of the rain!

It will be a guide—Kadman says laughing with the strength I have given him.

It begins to rain again. Standing against the pillar I must find the puddle or I shall drown in this desert expanding around me. I move through the opacity again(which first, the right? the left?)

5.

Is this why I have been brought here?
Another answer(I have been brought here!)

Stay here till you are dead or have escaped, finding your landmarks by the markings in your darkness—Kadman says, his voice distant now.
Still unable to hear if there is something new in my midst. My attempts at my intimacy, my legitimacy, my territoriality, are ambivalent(impossible to claim a first affirmation)this is one thing I
must. Affirm myself.

I have difficulty in screaming—I tell Kadman, so he will know(as if he did not and I were speaking to a stranger)

When the time comes, externalized or internalized, it does not matter. It is the scream that is important.
(a first affirmation)
I have grown
I have grown good
I have grown(too?)good at negotiating
even my passions.

Is this why I have been brought here?
Laughter and marijuana waft into the fecund dampness—Guide, is that you?
My lips plan to wrap around the tube, moistening, but there is no answer or it cannot possibly answer me even if an answer was had. Feeling the stone prison and my penis quickly to be sure I am still alive(always accustomed to touching my potentate)lending me strength. Otherwise I am flaccid, a shadow and I watch it carefully. An expansion of my definition: I am blood
(I am skin)

muscle
strings and tubes
and I am bone.
I(in this I lose faith)am capable of love

You have a soul—Kadman says

but I am no closer to it, given it
away as words.
Do I
Do I
Do I love
Do I love this
This black place?
(I rub my feet against one another and feel their soreness
remembering they have run directionless)
Mourning myself.
Yes! After surviving, I will always be of and from its black.
I smell Phoenix. I sat against her right buttock, noticing for another time just like the first time, its shape its curve her spine. I am very hard and am looking forward to her again, even if I fail again, too impatient to complete my ejaculation(I feel in danger within her)not sure and not one word dropped as to how well I have done; I rest my head on her labia—This—Phoenix outlines a circle with her legs, which I am sure is the world since her lips are its center—Is just a temporary fix and is needed each night to keep the numbness of your words distant.
dadududumddddadidududddddddddddadidadi dadi dadidydimdaddddimm—I listen to the rain against a roof.

A decision to avoid actions must be disregarded here—Kadman interjects.

Is that why I have been brought here?

You were never really brought here but found

this place after you had been here—Kadman murmurs—We judge each other by our preferences of smell, appearance(sometimes taste touch and sound)and by our own set of sins and non-sins. There is no logic in our judging—Kadman lets me wait, chortling.

Why should I want to be judged by you?

Because—A character in my head interdicts into this monologue—We haven't other judges here. First, you must render a judgment on yourself.

Reestablishing the statements I have made(those I have heard; those I have committed)Where might these recollections lead? I try to find a sound in boyhood scenes, but cannot(cannot find one I feel was in the air and not only in my head)If I separate statements I have said from those I have committed, where will I go?

dddddididid umdududumdimdimdimdimdaddddididi-didydydydududydidddddi

Rocking, I frantically try to find anyone and someone(any brick in my wall)to continue my emptying, to rest my eyes upon without recognition or the desire to understand—I will sit on your mind, wrestling from you the ability to fight, to make yourself heard(most of all to yourself)leaving you charred, like the raped, unable even to watch another human being for a long unabated time—Another character in my head says to another character in my head.

All I want to hear is the static and closing of stations before national anthems. I search for the repetition of a precipitating theme. Walking on my toes, my palms turned forward through another haze.

I don't have to do anything, inevitably, but die, Darling. No, not even respond—I say to the banter around me.

6.

Mother, pregnant and squatting, says to me—And is it time to arrive?—Smelling my sweat I begin to shiver, she begins to dissolve. I want to go beyond my voice; get behind it. I have stayed behind, marking lines that I can touch and feel as new features of the terrain.

I shall meet you again and at all times be with you—Kadman says from the unfound and coughs two or three hollow bursts then laughs. This darkness of the senses is a suffocation, smell here so overpowering, its acidity transforming me.

Divinity, will you speak to me again?—It is so wonderful, each time, to hear my voice—Are you here? Speak! It's my habit to believe that voices, forming human words, must originate from human beings.
Stretching my fingers
outward, I
I have played this game, carving another X from the silt.

But I couldn't
But I couldn't hear you
But I couldn't
But I couldn't hear
But I couldn't hear you
But I couldn't respond

if you were dead—He knows what I think till I scream for silence(anything better than not being able to hide)
Throwing stones in no definite direction one tossed across, hitting only the ground, no, wall(no)I still don't know how wide this place is, how far it reckons. I throw many and mettle rattles, the sounds giving me courage until I've run out of my few stones. I kiss my fingers, smell and taste the faint waif. Here, in the dust and soil,

excrement and vegetation, smelling my whole existence. Here the answer lies, in my hollowness someplace behind my organs. I make little swirls. It frightens me to lie down and still expend energy as If I were running. Am I? I was taught energy was necessary to move and assumed rooms always had exits(I can find none)

Stop looking at your wrists!

Why? I am locked here in this hollow other place—I pound my chest(Kadman will see)

This is the secret of your escape.

I have looked; in my blood dripping is my escape—I feel with my tongue my knuckle gnash.

In this commonplace it lies.

How?

Each has the same death and the same mortality—Kadman says and fades again.

So I am dead!

I did not say this—Kadman responds, holding each word in anger over my shoulder.

I take off my shoes to better feel this place and become this place, rubbing my feet across the tile, waiting to be cut or to feel something familiar. Avoiding the beginning of investigating my patterns(listen to my heartbeat)da-da da-da da-da da-da almost like the rain.

Kadman, I will soon shit in my pants! Is there a toilet around?

Does it matter in this place.

I assume I will eventually arrive at another wall or a door.

Is there anything which can be anything without limit, Kadman?

How should I know?

But I thought...

That I was in the know, a pal of God's—Kadman has a fit of laughter.

Don't laugh at me!

At your ignorance.

So, can there be anything greater than the limited?

We just can't know.

But if nothing is limitless

We're having impossible dreams.

But all things are made of energy and they bring along their decay.

Some things might not be and because they might not be, they are always with us.

How would such things be formed?

By what they might be.

So?

?

So then, I don't know where to go from here.

God, you are slow—Kadman's voice reeks.

I can feel it between my fingertips.

Your decay?

Is it my decaying?

Yes and what might be. It's all ours.

I walk quicker, swing my head, walk quicker.

FLATLANDS

1.

I search my mote liquid, slipping on another spot, my feet sore, blistering from their meanderings. A mouse or rat or other paws rush over my ankle, reminded of the insects around me. I recall Magrite's castle on a large boulder above a beach beneath an almost cloudless sky showing as of yet nothing of the ensuing hurricane. I step into some excrement, the flies buzz wildly.

Kadman, please, please wait for me! Let me go!

I am not your imprisoner. I don't have control of your release.

Then you too are a prisoner. Where were you before and where will you be after this?

What before and after? I've been here with you. I am not in a place you aren't or haven't been, or could not be. What befores and afters do you mean?

Who will answer my prayers without all this flight!

Why, yourself. Please don't lose your cool. You always need to retrace from that—Kadman entreats to calm me, acting the ignorant for a moment in our relationship, inverting—You must keep your cool, so I can succeed—He lies.

Where am I?—I ask of the ground without hope for an answer.

In this catacomb—Kadman prays incoherently for my strength while I search for a light to pretend is sunlight.

A urinal

A catacomb

A tomb

A temple.

Quiet! Shut up! Why won't you give me a straight answer?

You don't want one. My words are what you expect to hear.

Why can't I find you? Why won't you let me?

You have just begun to search.

I listen to the splashing of water each step I take, my feet cold and surrounded, wading my way deeper. Splashing my face with this water, removing my soil as a beginning(even my excrement must be swept aside)sins and virtues flushed with the water of the rain(tempted to drink, I touch my lips with it)Counting my ribs, thirteen, twelve, eleven, ten, nine, eight, seven, six, five, four, three, two, one, my iliac crest and abdominal wall, my hip bones severely outlined(I touch my visitor)

I am trapped—I say.

How could you make this mistake after all this time? You've tried your best not to lie to yourself, as I recall.

I am trapped, it does not matter how—I lie, smoke another pretend cigarette. Pretending to know me.

Drawn down to Phoenix's hips, received dydydydiddid dududadudaddddddddddddddddi
tddudududududumdidididymdydydydydydymdidud dydydydymdidadadudududumdydide

Fallen into a breach with one two-thousand year old acacia tree desperately clinging.—Where was this?—Kadman asks from the shadows, showing me a picture, in which I do not know the other—Who is that?—I ask, listening to Kadman's laughter—Why don't be silly, that's you—I begin to resurface(the pressure in my brain subsiding)I hear, in this catacomb, rejoicings echoing about me, flat hand splattering and skirting from the center of a skin, an underwater explosion its ripples continuing outward in ever widening circles, drawing me to my edge, a clan split and it's sinews exposed. I see an outline ahead(is it Kadman?)it seems to be rocking and praying. Dovening repeated Dovening.

I believe I am going the right way—I repeat unconvinced—Kadman, I believe I am going the right way?—Tripping on an uneven surface, I receive no response, falling through spider webbings and thrashing, the night sounds of nature, the scent of swamps and the unwashed, the hills made by red ants, the touch of cicadas, crickets and beetles.

What is the answer?—I have touched and seen only stones, silt and insects, left my shoreline behind, my assumption that what was stepped on is still behind and what will be stepped on is still ahead, the lines I've drawn on the muddied tile(underneath all our
stones)a search for security
Tic-tac-toe. I'm X and play myself and still Y wins.
My air full of flies giving seed to maggots.

2.

You must unearth yourself.

But this place is confusing, inextricable relations. I sit where my feet have carried me, and try to dream of the climb remaining before

returning.

Brought up to fear the unknown and to be terrified of what is unknowable(mothers and fathers)rather than continue into our ignorance. Unless we need to survive.

This place you came from—Kadman says.

All I have unearthed is this hole I am bound with, no images but the pebbles beneath my hands to use as a trial, living impotently for the rest of my days—This I barely speak so quiet in order not to hear myself(another laughable idea)Mark another line on the tile.

But my marks do not place their hold.

I stop descending, for it is indefinite. We are afraid of the indefinite, so we will not pursue indefinite things.

We must speak.

Speak of what?

Of absurdities.

Absurdities are a waste of time. We must speak of where we are.

In your dreams?

A waste of...I'm not sure.

But certain dreams cannot be described.

Some of the indescribable?

Till words become deeds(as with certain religious people)

It is only by throwing this aside and passing your text that you can go on—Kadman speaks.

Follow me a hand beckons.

Phoenix said—I have felt the deadening tension in your

penis, its loss of size as it remains inside me. I have felt your attempts(
To find my way deeper and deeper
into my groin
I have felt my attempts
to leave me
and to climb
(as long as I can with my bare hands)
leaving this situation
believing in new circumstances
I have felt my attempts
to trust in the voices that speak to me
without body
I have witnessed my attempts to find them
(I must go today)
I climb, striding with a power I haven't seen before(leaving my patterns behind)

You have decided to go? Go?

To where?—I ask before it passes.

The place you came from without—Kadman says. But that place is confusing, inextricable relations. I continue to hear the climb before me.
Follow me the hand beckons.
I Go.

3.

Listening to voices behind my ears, cricket-chimes crowding together for the end of a dialogue and an action. I am part of their dialogue but can only wait for their action and imagine(I have not seen or found them yet)My chills begin and pull; I hug myself, the rest of this place
as cold as myself.
This place
This place is
is a part of my...
I cling to this space of selfcreated boundaries(but walls can also aid the discovery of certain truths through limitation)It is time I learn this niche I am in. I look around the blindness and sniff the tile full of decomposing silt.
This place is a part of my...

Our soul—Kadman interrupts in my ear.

This place is a part of our soul—I answer, breathing in each new line.
This place has been and is a reenactment whose chain can't be broken. Once begun.

Once begun?—I am alive with the question.

It may never end for you—He says, my Shaman.

My God—I say low because I wish I could not hear myself. It may never end for you—Enough! Be rid of this place!

These things.
Uncover my internal hiding!
Stop this.
Uncover this.
enough.

I will become convalescent.

4.

In the more inclusive darkness of closed eyes I can see Phoenix standing, naked, hands covering her face—Do you think of me as an open mouth?—She walks into me—Where do I take you?—In the darkness of my fall I find another shell, trying to study its texture(I do not see it in my hands, but run my fingers across it)of a cracked bone. Through my fingertips I reach onward—I have a piece of your paradise now. Om-Ni-Pa. C'mon, just a little longer now—My panting has an edge, as if I am at its limit. Sitting atop my hips—Just sway back and forth with the metronome. Caress my chest. Yes. That small movement is like the vibration of my breath—Her nipples twisted between my fingers, her incantation helping me remember—Begin swaying again and again; keep the same rhythm and you will be set free—I am envious at how she can give her whole being to kisses about my genitals(I am incapable of becoming lost in her abscess)I feel her embrace and begin to undulate east to west(still see no light from her tunnel)looking for the door or the window or the crack in the wall or the way I must have come(her hole much too small yet(I have not made it big enough(east to west)I am sure I am lost, not sure that I entered this place at all.

What face have I?—I ask her.

I hear metal clinking and a fire's cackling, directionless. I masturbate in the hopes of exhaustion and the freedom that comes with it, but with my juice and smell come blood. Her legs spiral in little circles, accentuating her life.

I have decided she means the world.

I whisper to my birth(but I do not know if Kadman listens)the darkness lies in my head(whispering all this so

I can be assured of hearing what I think)a ludicrous idea, to believe I could hear everything I think if I whisper. There is too much lost to whispers. To have faith is to gain intuition, or to have intuition is to gain faith? I need a faith. Are they both spontaneous? Without permanence through knowing or permanence through accepting the unknowable
I just unhinge.
I jungle my coins, dull and clamping.
A large waterbug or mouse scurries along the edge of my heal.
A wisp.
Forced from the cocoon of the monologue,
I wonder if I can
survive a dialogue.
I feel resignation upon me.
Without thinking on it, I scatter.
Two cicadas copulate, awaken me to the space still necessary to traverse in this catacomb. I move toward their copulation, their wings vibrating in the open. Reestablishing my wonder at this(I hear Phoenix have an orgasm while clenching my rock and a cicada coming—I have a piece of your paradise now. Paradise can be found in things other than orgasm, our energies exhumed. Here, let me wipe it away for you—She begins wiping away the head of my penis.
Who did I hear?

I—Kadman again—Who else could be here?

I want to grab you, to ask who I am in this place—I yell to Kadman or to my guide or to anyone who might hear but(now that I've opened my eyes)no one will answer.

Are you here? I'm convinced I'm not sure of anything. I've lost all faith in my senses.

There is another place to start from.

Is this the place?—I laugh till I feel pain because I need to feel pain.

You need principles.

What do I need principles for?

Sperm rushing irresistibly to their egg—Kadman peels out.

I wade ankle deep into the water, splash my chest and submerge the top of my head, as a reassurance that I can live after this(as if I am baptized)I hope for continued rain as a reassurance of my past
to remain alive
bread and water
to avoid suicide.

I advance to find my numbers(because it is something to begin from)to find my head
scrape my knuckle against the tile, my blood comforting, falling onto the tile each arc of a slowly set metronome. I try to fall past meandering, but I cannot reach far enough down to refind the silence.

We must keep speaking to ourselves
each other
ourselves.

No place to disappear into, Kadman. I can't conjure it! I can't conjure it!

Finally, it is a necessity. Unable to avert my eyes, although I still attempt not to see. My old patternings, running from seeing
my beginnings near, near the end; splashing my face repetitiously to clear my mind and find temporary forgetfulness, not to think; to form patterns, stalactites in a cave, as long as a thought's full length. Unable to avert my eyes.

I squat, shit weakly; filled with liquid, I am empty.

I continue to move in the direction I've always moved, ever widening concentric circles.

5.

Laughing into this land, in preparation for my travels over the brackish and invisible waters. I remember the tomes and gestures of my voice as I look into the jars of my organs, continue onward, a need to be caressed.
Tripping over a wooden plank, I come across something new. Someone must have left this here, a device to scourge(through the flagellation and bleeding and headaches that have come)to grip through the waters.
Moving through uncharted places.
Religiously, I collect my remaining energy.

You should sometimes accept me, imbue yourself of me—Kadman says—We are all in it together.
I have felt genitals, a firefly whose light is not enough during its momentary flush. This is all. I hear water dripping(the rain has stopped again except for occasional raps)breaking the heavy air as I wave my arms about.

Even locusts would die more quickly in a place like this. Aren't I right Kadman? When I repeated my social security number last time, you said mother, father and us. What did you mean?
I have yet to give up the others I cannot find passing me, pregnantly pausing without touch without taste without listening without a glance without even a casual sniff(even their pores of skin do not inhale me)I listen to some scraping in an unknown pattern on the concrete, its sound increasing, producing a break in this din.

Wait. Which way have we gone?—But Kadman doesn't answer.
I rush down steps, down elevators down cliffs, through this unmapped corridor full of a catacomb. I am afraid of growing old down this hole(this to be my home)Flapping my arms, I try to fly, the darkness ahead

of me so thick(Mother and three others squat down and begin to work on their shape again, across a long stretch of sand)I stretch my hands through them and wave them about.
Canting through this swamp, am I at the beginning of an infinite terrain?
This is impossible. I throw stones and hear rattling, but this does not show an end. Infinite(only maybe infinite to the west)until it reaches back to me, or to behind the wall that was my first shore. Before me? I can recognize smells and insects, the mortar and silt, du dadum du du dudam da du du da dddda dumdududu another splash(there is a hole somewhere in this place to the outside and perhaps I can fit through it like water)I should find the water and let it drip onto my face, the sounds of cicadas, grasshoppers, crickets, and occasional sightings of fireflies. I hear a mosquito hovering, looking for warmth in blood.
I imagine I
I imagine I am
I imagine I am being
I imagine I am being suffocated in a pool of water
and strangling The Kadman, both of us dying without air.
Why is dreaming so difficult for me suddenly?
I assume Kadman's voice to originate from a man.
I assume I will be fine(but not really
until the sun of this place finally returns)
I assume this place has a sun.
To assume anything is to chance error while not to leaves me no customary beginning, no first step, on a carousel. To say no is necessary(it sticks and cannot be gotten rid of)to look for the essential hidden behind each pattern which hides, habits formed to keep the peace. Can I find

habits to keep my peace?

I will go mad without some habit!

Stop groping your way. I am tired of your games—My guide begins—Where are you? Where?—He passes on, mumbling—Where?

Somewhere in this place.

As it is, you've made a mess of things.

I blame my penis—Its inability to stop its desires. Condemnation lies in these languid charted places, that portion of me which is traversed, not wanting to attempt to find the virgin soil. I can finally hear Kadman breathe(another breath)synchronized with mine(I assume it is Kadman's)and this thought frightens me. Can this be the first time he has breathed? Have I heard it before? I believed Kadman didn't need to breathe.

Kadman, do you breathe?

Lying down with my ears against my knees, the water soaks my butt. I feel my dwindling in shivers run out from me. I see no shapes and no sky. I can imagine only blindness, have lost all my customs of time or space. I feel hollow, not able to view star systems in a sky. Finding my heartbeat, I begin toward that, following the rain my beating

d d du d dum d du d d du d dum d du d d du d du d du d d d di du d d d di du dum

Following scenes in which I no longer feel a part, I sneeze, rock, reestablish an emotion, certain facts, doubts of my commitment(I no longer judge truthfulness)These recollections are only a stage. Even if I begin to believe in them, will I be ready? Is this all we have?

We are a stranger in our own land. We must reestablish our times. Become detoxified—Kadman adds while I feel what it is like to straighten my back again, as if the feeling will carry me.

It will take too long.
Too long for what?
For the number of my days.
What else can we do?—Kadman asks rhetorically.
The internal dialogue must be clear, clearer than these illusions I play with, eventually seen through to
To...
didididididadumdi dumdidumdidu di dy dup dup dup dup didi dip Glass didididadumdi dumdidumdidu di dy dup dup dup dup didi dip
dip dup didididup dady dade dade dadedididumdum didi di di di bottom
di dup dade dade dup boats
dididi Finding another puddle, I stamp into its middle, listening to each plish until one drop rises as far as my face, restoring flute notes through my blood, its flow radiating inward through my darkening red pool. Soon I will be drunk, feasts of my legacy.
If I reconstruct something, it can become a vision of the past, if I recapitulate this scene, then it no longer is the past, the past as finally a rushing toward the future. It is not important to know that I will finish, but what I will have where I am rushing(I must get out from this pyramid's perimeters in order to survive(even if it is a chance at death))My compass spins violently, roughly carrying me askew. I look for Phoenix's slash, used as a forgetfulness, as a sensation to forget all other sensations, despairingly, for the seconds of my orgasm. Twisting, she arched her back five times in our first night's twist(repetitions? Only repetition?)A union. Must every inception be the death of something? Lost in a search for our inception.

You've assumed your answers. Already fixed—Kadman responds—But don't you think I could prove you wrong? We begin with your accusation.

No, no, let's forget that. As long as you're here, you can't claim my birth.

Then with your assumption that a god exists.

The past. It exists no longer—I reclaim, but he will not stop laughing till I hold my ears(for the first time I do not want to hear his sounds)—We assume escape because We cannot accept our eventual demise—My guide flourishes his hand(it flashes in the darkness)an arc like a flapping fish—You should accept it, because then your struggle would cease—Another first step(I must be passionless in my ascension)

And will you ascend?—Kadman questions. Realizing that this is the first time Kadman has asked me a question I am expected to answer, my mouth goes dry and my abdomen tightens—Will We meet?

How, if I descend and you ascend? Unless this universe is a giant sphere. Then we might still meet.

6.

Continuing to look for the card, a something to do. Habits so as to forget, so as to make my time easier here. Habits of thought are the most sleep inducing, for they induce assumptions and repetitions. Habit of change is another repetition, continual movement, not having to sit and contemplate.

But we will go mad, Kadman, without some habits as markers. Please let me fuck you, Kadman.

I remain with you in this space and wait to revive something I've already had many times, and this is what I get?

Why do you want something you've already had?

It's exposing new bone, anticipation of new organs, a danger, all primal thoughts are reawakened. Why do you chase it so much?
Having drunk woman's milk, I am still unrefreshed.

I would offer to carry you but I can only lift you with your help—Kadman says—Do you recognize me yet?—Finishing, Kadman waves from someplace ahead or behind I cannot tell. I seem unable to believe in where we are. Pressing on, stumbling, hesitating and continuing after intervals, I try to decide if this is the path to an end. Birds' shadows crisscross, creating illusionary interstices against the navy blue
water.

We know the strength that can come of obsession—A voice says whose name is known but I can't think of it.

I wonder why I have forgotten your name. Could you tell me?—I am anxious over this forgetting.

It is unnecessary. You know it.

Yes. Now I recall. It is Kadman.

Caught in my disconnected past, recollecting specks, each dissipating speck uncovering a cool lime green, inhaling and exhaling, its waves tapping rhythms of spaces I have not discovered, remembering some days, others blending into one which becomes many, continuing my submerging, each square inch of my skin. Taking in all the air I can manage, expanding my chest, I try to set one foot before the other without faltering. I am ready(in case I
submerge
I can hold my breath almost two minutes)Eventually, I will remember each day(I pray this is a way)I will become able to decide
what happened in my chosen days, my history, steps constrained and cautious dwindling time. Am I too meticulous in this recant? The becoming is what I seed.
Can I spare the energy to continue the climb?(not away but out)Beginning within my testicles, I try to travel through my system to my head(lying in wait)breathing(right to left testicle)Waiting. Swallowing my breathless secretions, I wait, but none resurfaces. Only sweat, my scrotum's rocking, collecting my energy and wait till it isn't possible to withhold. I must trace a trail through my system. I spill into my stomach, forcing my lungs to exhale, trying to find a trial.

Have you decided to be alone? Or to conserve? Or, in fear, to go back, or to join us ahead?—Kadman asks. Unsure of how to answer, I put my left foot before my right in the semblance of an answer.

7.

After I take three breaths, I know what I will do, constructing the existence of events before this, like remembering a fugue heard long enough ago that the remembrance creates a new score.

This place

This place is

This place is a part of my...

Our soul—Kadman interrupts in my ear.

Scratching my acne-ridden face, sniffing at each finger's acquired odor(a habit)I am sure of the necessity of this moment although it may not matter where(since I still do not know where now is)my ignorance of it no longer frightening for I feel close to it(almost safe in it)I've begun to rely on my physical senses again, ill and limited as time. With my imagining I can go farther(perhaps too far)And am afraid of the edge. It is a habit to avoid the edge or to press to it and beyond, not to it and remain. This will show of what metal I am made. I assume I am; I think; for without these assumptions, I cannot go onward(in any objective way I am lost because I cannot be objective)none of us can, peering onward.

This place is a part of our soul—I repeat, breathing in each new line to reaffirm it and my expansion.

It is resolved—Kadman ends—Are you afraid of touching God or growing old?—Kadman conspires.

What god?

Me—Kadman says.

You cannot be a god. A god would not have to wait till he had the strength to tell me if I should survive—I say(hearing my echo)Overjoyed at my remembrance.

A god would not need to tell you anything. He

could not be seen but hear
could not be found, but find
could not be hunted, but hunt...

Enough! Be rid of these things!
Uncover my internal hiding!
I cannot.
Why?
Because the same could be Man.
Are you?—I ask.

I receive no reply. I cannot believe, believing in my isolation. It is too difficult to wait while I count the time, vociferous and alone.

Goddamn you Kadman! Give me a judgment now! I need your judgment first!(crying, I taste my tears and am so glad I can still cry)—I'll even call you God—yet receive no reply.

My feet slap stone in the direction I've accepted as ahead. I look out toward me and can feel myself running, can hear myself heaving, as if I am not a part of this.

FOOTHILLS

1.

Before a mountain, its top beyond sight, pumice lays broken, strewn, and powdered from winds and rains, shallow furrows cut across by hundreds of thousands of feet climbing with little break. I pick up a piece of the stone, dusty and sharp. Dropped, it breaks into two unequal parts, one small and diamond shaped, the other a jagged distorted parallelogram. The sun hovers behind the mountain, unseen from the beginning. One man, his penis hard(due to his hand)strokes a woman's clitoris, waiting for her desire and preparing so that he can insert it, but it will soften by then because the woman concentrates only on sky. She reminds me of a catatonia because he shakes her, calls to her, finally in a paroxysm of frustration he slaps her, holding his deadened desire up to watch it shrink, he blames her, will blame her, holding his deadened desire
he will watch it shrink and in a paroxysm of frustration he will slap her, call to her, finally he will shake her and he will do this with every woman he will desire. But she doesn't move, until the blame, then she takes him in, very businesslike, her arms folded around his waist, his fingers imbedded in her buttocks, thudding against her ribs, pushing her back against the bench as she begins to murmur for the first time, asking him to calm.
I know this because this was our pattern.

Church bells peel in this hole, an incessant chorus which will not stop, all other sounds nullified, as if my death or my resurrection has been announced(only one? Which?)the funeral procession pauses having had an altercation with a red car, the red car disturbing their lamentation, dividing it in two—Wait! We must give them time, death has the right of way—A boy says, as if to a celebration, rattling a rattler, wearing a tuxedo, and very upset. A man, wearing a frayed black canvas mourning dress and crepe half-veil, keens, teeth receding as he draws his lips back unstraight, while other mourners reflect upon a chance reflected upon earlier and so become weaker and weaker as
this chance becomes all their memories and possibilities.
I grab him, feel no texture, only his skin in my lungs, expanding like filling leather water bags.

Who are you?—I say while moving toward the Keening-man.

I am your mourning and mourner—He spits onto the stone, touching his veil, brushing his sweat beneath it.

I rush to uncover the accident victim, to see if I am also involved. My temples pound(a peek at my heart)racing in anticipation of when I will see his head. I try to recreate what I might be(inside this sarcophagus)perhaps just hopes.

Raising the veil I find that he is myself waiting.

I turn, doven, rush(in the abstract peak's direction)climbing to a peak I have had no proof of, just because I am inclined to believe in ends of climbs, finding my direction by some unknown trek, needing to discover the walkway before I pass its markers, before its furrows fill and I have to make new ones. Remembering, reassembling, recalling

recollecting. Dizzying.
It is in the proof we must live.
We can do no more but dream.
Surveying the foot of the mountain, I find no one else.
A light crosses my face, awakening atrophied pores, tingling, on a sliver of air, disappearing as fast as I take one breath. There is a hole! There is a draft! There is a light!
Like a child I catch the water and throw it into the air, droplets hitting my face(reminded of my flesh)

There is more, you are nearing a return—Kadman says.
I feel my face wet in my hands.
I want to begin burying my useless parts. Why has this become a show? Let's finish this!
Mother sits by me, her head freshly shaven(Sephira has grown old since my beginning)—Is it like what is received from our groins? Strung for a few precarious moments? An ambitious response in some pitch black tunnel—I press my hands against the wrinkles on her forehead till I feel her skull, pretending to become lost in what she feels and thinks(I laugh quietly and sadly still)
I am afraid to move, afraid to scream because I recall that these tellings bare me, leave my location found, afraid of finishing because to do so begins another replication—I am so tired—Sephira says—Of your immobility. I will not remain with you any longer—She removes my hands. Her skull revealed beneath my palms, its fragments clinging to my hands, even as I circularly rub them against my soiled clothes to scrape away her imprint. Searching the ground for leaches(moving further along the slope)to where the light comes.
I do not know my way back now(trying to begin my bloodletting)
Returning to his hearse, the boy bangs his knee against

the door, cradling over from the day and the pain. I follow the procession in my canvas and veil, muttering incomprehensibly low(for no others)occasionally hearing myself—What parts are missing? What?
For some years, I tried to create a vagina with paint. I took hold of mine, smeared a slit of black paint in a distorted and messy lip. Missing a womb, I painted on my belly an orb. I felt naked with this hole, my house bespeckled(too unkempt and chaotic)full of faces, each profile distorting into another group of many faces, contriving my fate(as if each movement of my muscle were changes, another organism.
I am always cold of late, the slowing of my blood, hesitant to respond, to commit. I cannot resist holding others responsible, a hardening of my blood(words escalating in speed)with the ice that holds my intimate parts in check. I create an event to feel heartache, the truth unimportant, just the scars. I require tragedy in my life to make myself more interested in it, others more sympathetic. The pain from our forebears, the dizziness, the shakes from our cuts. When all my things are in their place within my house, I will still not be able to articulate a thing I have learned.

This can only be intuitive—is repeated, but I cannot trust intuition. I stop, falling behind my words.

Why are you searching for corpses here?—Kadman asks.

Are there no dead?

Our present—Kadman answers(I have reached his outline finally)he is as tall as me—Our past.

Time and generations?—I ask.

Would there be a future if these were the dead?—Kadman spits at me. I see his words eject from his lips, disappear, then land near.

The future does not, by its definition, require a past generation—I am almost smug.

No, but without it, no future would be. There would be no beginning—I wonder if Kadman could die(as if this could be or bring me peace)

You assume there is a beginning—I say.

Do you believe we resume, eternally, the past. Repetitions? It is too easy this way to give up responsibility. We can blame too much away on fate—Kadman reads my thoughts, then continues—That you even wondered if I could die endangers your escape. You will have to find me again—His outline disappears.

Judged by results, not by what has been sacrificed to arrive!—I yell, laughing over the words I am capable of speaking in this place, searching for liars and ticks in my pubic hair.

Look down. Here is the key, not a god which has ascended too far to understand primordial dust—Kadman cants till I am forced.

Shutup, Be quiet! My ears hurt with your incantation!

The key is here, in this hole of urine and excrement and... Here, take it! Find It!

My guide jumps across the darkness, biting my nose, my nostrils buried within his mouth(I smell its scent)withdrawing my face—What are you doing!—Don't you recognize your smell!—It shouts, beginning to move away, a dissipating gas.

Why did you bite my nose?—But I enjoyed its scent and feel.

It'll feel no different from all the other times.

Times? What feel?

Can't you feel the direction you take?—It or I say, confused—It was here before we were born—His form losing additional gas, translucent.

No! It can't be. We can't have existed eternally!

What about eternity? What was I exhaling about?—My guide dissipates up the slope—I am not impressed with your zeal. It doesn't seem sincere. You must believe sincerely and have faith for a project to be successful. It can really be cast aside only once—Kadman returns(each time he speaks, it is a returning)as if he was not here before.

I find a staircase(finally! Have I found a doorway?)

I am afraid of these eternal possibilities, propagation of thoughts, a reincarnation of names. If it is in this place old as Woman, the beginning, but I am frozen in my repetition of one, a prayer, atonal(without change(a film running again and again)I doven and listen to the water-like hum then, collecting myself, I try to step. Again and again. Here! Another stair!(my God? Will it be another bricked-up wall?)Beginning to climb it, I find, past the first two steps

a fork. Should I go right or left? Westerly or Easterly?

Kadman, which way do I go? Which way do I go now! Goddamn you!

Quickening, a child indulges in the newness of life, hammers a xylophone, a beckoning image of hope(his eyes still not focusing)I close my eyes through another time crawling up another stair, coming closer to my shaman(or does he still move remaining equidistant with me?)within me the child unceasingly strikes the slats fifty times, listening to each eruption gleefully, its urgency, each repetition unique, a spectacle(grasping the air to grasp it, for one breath's length, as if I can start my heart)I feel another stair.

Crawling like a cat, belly down, I search for

my drug.

2.

Another stair climbed(another stone picked up)I try to decipher its striations, sienna and its burning. I am fascinated that a world, with color, can be seen again(I pick it up and throw it upward, ahead of me)Watch the darkness, waiting for its descent, hearing it crash, somewhere above(and ahead)It does not come
back to me.
I try to fall asleep so that I might wake up and, for a confused moment, be as I was before this place(or dream what is later)but neither of these is a possibility. I am forced to keep moving(another step and the fall below me growing greater)Unsure about every step I crawl upward, looking back for my sticks(with my head low, as close to the floor as possible)I see lines(I am not sure how many, if they are mine or if they are seen)there is a dispersed band of light here
a sun of some sort growing.
Have I arrived to the morning?
Looking, I see the victim's prone figure in this place, as if it were dead, my head off to the right upon the floor.
My Eve comes out of the darkness and grabs hold my dissipation.
My steps a reply, I put my feet end to end. I still can measure! I have measured twelve inches of it. It is no longer so immeasurable.
I have smelled urea and shit
I have heard mosquitoes, crickets and flies, have felt the silverfish and have seen the lightning bug.
I have felt damp mortar
I have bled
I have heard rain
I have found light

I have lost tic-tac-toe
against myself
I have thrown stones which have hit future ground.
Now I have a definition of this place. Am I any better for it?
I hope the place above answers to a consistency(even this place was consistent)our purgatory. If something is counted, its images repeated, it will reach the deepest memory, a way into the dialogue and with it a set of rules(a permanence of illusion again)Believing above has to at least be found consistent, I try to recount the sticks, each number paused and lengthy. I attempt to feel another step(another dead end?)
Sticky, wringing my hands to resist grasping for a next ledge. My eyes remain downward.
We are(no)We are not

We are not chained—I lift my hands to the sixth step(it is time to run from the tradition of this hole)seeking turbulence.
I accept these recently discovered links.
As I walk toward Kadman's last few words, another fly races by. I touch its mark upon my cheek.
dum du dum du du dudumdu dadudumddudumd-ddddddadddadumdudddd
I can hear the rain splashing somewhere near. Now I know that something is near. Tongue gliding along lips, I wave my hands about, feeling their turmoil, but am unable to find them. Kadman and the rain. I pick sand from my toes and try to imagine the Atlantic ocean lap, but I fall back, tenuously holding on to a squat.

Does this lover care?—She draws away pulling her armpit from my tongue—I'm afraid you're not worthy, you're too snug and warm and too apt to produce life—after a pause continuing—I have history in my

groin and your inability to pursue it has put you in this lowliness.
Panting on this treadmill, I am not sure where my future and present sit, far apart or close. I open my eyes, drawn back from Phoenix's touch, but still cannot find her, as illusive as when I am blind(I am the only thing real in my circumstances)Oh, animal, my belly is beginning to hurt(the card only a direction)I wonder if I will find a toilet(that would be a growing relief)I wonder if it'll be soon? I wonder if there will be toilet paper.

We should sit and talk about this, these memories you've rebuilt—Kadman says.
Memories of my exposure
since my circumcision
of my nakedness
my franticness.
Not to trust my private parts.
Memories of denial
denial of faith
denial of objects of faith
(to practice faiths)
of wanting to continue my name
my seed.
To overcome myself
to shatter myself
a tiny genetic part of myself.
Not to discover myself unless happenstance
(my ghosts in this happenstance
the cleavage of my ghosts)
Memories of my exposure
(with you)
undressings
Memories of my denials
my desires

of fleeing from above and below.
since my circumcision
(Trapped on this stairway, my conundrum the answer to itself)

Here!

Attempting to slow my exposure, I try to stop and not continue, trapped in this stairwell between two ends. I wonder where I should go.
Where can I continue?
I must run if I am ever to reaproach those squatting in the distance, waking.
I have been here for an unknown amount of time, an eye boggling number of sticks, shivering and uncovered in this cell. What crimes have I been sentenced for?(As if my sentence is over only because of my hope)How was my body discovered? Beginning at my oily forehead, down to my chest(pinching my tits)my abdomen and navel, and finally, after spine's curvature, buttocks and thigh, holding my penis(holding onto a fetal position)I feel a band of power within my groin expanding(I must reestablish what I am like, whether I am appealing, the feel of vital muscle)Without my body's memory, I am lost. This energy is finally received from my groin in a stream made of fish.

Am I empty, Kadman?

I've only grasped that which I was taught and nothing more(I was taught to listen but not to hear)I am lost even though I have learned I am lost. If I awoke, never seeing the earth again I would often feel its dance spiralling, repeating subito a dream at me, a beginning of an obsession to reach it, it would never let me live(it does not even let me be now)Imagining pictures of oceans and continents and their twisting, I sit and concentrate on a landing. For the first time I am unable to hide in a state-

ment of impotence.
Pulling the sheet more tightly against her breasts, Phoenix tried to hide them, so sharp and asymmetrically poised under bright lights—What do you think of my breasts, Stone?—In a different place, I turn—What do you think of my breasts, Stone?—Lying quietly in the darkness, wondering where she is—What's better than thinking of my breasts? What do you think of my breasts?—They're tight and pointed and cut my lips in exhilaration, but shouldn't you know about your own breasts?—You ask me the same of your—She touched my genitals—When you're undressed. I believe you're here because I knew you would pass—Phoenix said—Letting my limp penis fall—You can forget everything, but—Phoenix's nipples enraged, elongated and hard with the anticipation of her orgasm—First you have to force each nipple to a purple delirious—When is a nipple delirious?—Have you ever truly tried to be worthy of a woman's hips?—Baring her teeth, she laughed three times. I have no hope because I am too weak to resist my desire for her (we don't know where or how to escape or stop)this need for orgasm with her and its high is my downfall(if I can deny this place away, then I'll have her)Kissing her collar bone because it can easily be broken.
Unsure of I before I was eight, except when in first grade, watching the stoneskinnedandhaired teacher with power teach us, because I can't recollect an emotion(here is my place to start, this teacher)I recollect feelings I'd never forgotten. Here I can recapitulate the habit of time.

Am I falling away?—The ground scummy under my fingers—Am I dreaming?—but I am here again, the muck peeling—Kadman, wouldn't you rather play a game, not just sleep?

How do you know I am just sleeping?

Wouldn't you like to play a game?

Then play—but nothing arrives—Begin.

But what game?—Again, after a time—Kadman? Kadman, what game? I want to see and touch you!—Stretching to reach the sound of his voice, slapping at his darkness. Unable to wait for his reply, I search, trying to feel the space I cannot see—I need a flashlight!

You will not find me here

Where is here?

One of several places. A urinal, a catacomb...

A tomb!

I wasn't allowed to finish.

Children can mingle everything(because they are new)If a thing doesn't fit they feel it will eventually so they wait. If only I were a child, regaining this ability to wait for my fit(that shall be my conquest, to reach that source again, burried)but am only able to concentrate on my next move, already predicated(Am I being punished?)I must escape from this place, this pull—Can't I only clutch onto you? This can be too quiet a place—I whisper to create sound and it doesn't echo a response(I hope it is only a dream of a quiet place without echoes
or responses)this place should at least be small, it would not be so much a prison that way; I try to remember steps or doors or exits again, scraping the ground with my left hand's fingernails(my right hand pushed into my abdomen to clot)a shiver through my skeleton(to find some history lost in the pebbles. An inestimably removed familiar object is my quest(the card a beginning)

Have you copied my birth certificate yet?

Copied your birth certificate?

You've stolen it!

Why would I need it?

To become me, you thief!

You've got it backwards. You become me. Thinking of searching is a mistake. To stop is a mistake. This leaves me only with the search. I hear a fly buzz around from where I began. Could it be me(the fly's away)Weltering.

Go on and see how far it has gone.

I move toward the sound of the whirling fly.

Thief! You've locked me in here so you could take on my identity.

You'll castrate yourself if you continue on.

I am castrated. I feel the pain, Kadman.

I don't have it. You probably dropped it in the dark. It's back where you started I'm talking about. You've masturbated too much and tried to be something unheard from. You've also tried to reach something impossible.

What is that?

The purity of indifference. Such does not exist.

Am I seeking indifference?

If you keep glancing at your veins, perhaps you are seeking death. Go on—I do not because I am not sure what to hold.

Stop! I want you to stop!—I say

But stop what, Adam?

I spit and hear the spit land—I told you to stop! Stop staring at me, you ugly bastard! Stop looking at me as if your thoughts encompass me!—I climb, my open palms rippling tiny exploratory pools, small points in an ocean. I begin to wonder if I can swim.

I believe for a moment I am buried in a cow pasture, recognize the stench of my particles of scent, like Raflesia Arnoldi as it dies. I can not even find a sharp object. (What would I do if I found it?)

I grasp another pebble tensely, found on the seventh stair and bring it to my lips. kissing it, warily watching to and fro lest anyone see, awash in more shadows. Kadman, I must not forget to catch up with Kadman. I have gained a little strength, through my kiss, a stone tossed to where I will go(I will find it again as hope)

3.

Rushing across this wilderness, flight necessary from this...this conundrum, my head turned extremely right, but still impossible to see behind me(I need mirrors and mirages)I must study my backside so I can learn to see behind.

Why do you move away, Kadman? Why?—I ask the sound of steps ahead of me(I choose to believe in a direction)—Why do you move away? I'm only seeking the right place to learn a new incantation. Kadman? Will I get to this place?

Your happiness all part of a chain of historical events which you imagine to be your savior—He laughs—Who could be your god?—Patting me on the head as I would a dog he asks—What could be your god?—When we no longer have gods, growth can begin from our necessities and our incompleteness again—Everyday—He says—We seek ours. Did you not forget to bring it? Did you not forget to bring it?—Flicking his wrist and laughing huskily and slowly, his eyes memorize something I do not see ahead of me(I am afraid to look into them)I can imagine recognizing the depth of his search within my own eyes.

Pushing my palm to my lips, I kiss it, still dressed in my mourning.

Hope

caresses my groin, growing. I am a man again, with a narrow definition.

The responsibilities of our first breach.

of our first circumcision(walking with pain

between our legs)I am bowed down(in this breath)before a maker or a

first ancestor forged in a fire before our time.

That's what I am—Kadman says, but I do not understand what is meant.
(I pray inexhaustibly to myself)
One can only pray(to another)for safety
(I bow down to myself)
One must find fervency and faith
(I am religiously fervent in a denial of faith)
Breathing within such a tiny space, my penis and testicles constrict, prepare another reservoir, as gods, pearls swimming within my sack. My head beneath my armpits(licking with
a cat's lick)I taste my saltiness.

I am hungry—Becoming obsessed with this necessity, the recollection of my mortality, the first requirement of creation, my feeding or my decimation. I inhale the air of my armpits—Can you smell the lilacs?—Phoenix asked(what lilacs can I smell?)The air full of her sexual evidence, increasing in vivacity
adding density to this unidentifiable ground.
Prattling around an ever widening diameter(I have decided to approach my space in a widening spiral)circles without knowledge. Wanting to feel the pain of a muscle extended as far as it can without snapping, bending till my palms touch the ground. I bounce back quickly with satisfaction reveling in this completion. I jump and am hoarse(it echoes)I echoed. I echo. I bite my forearm, almost puncturing my skin, till it nearly begs in pain, to feel flushed, warmth rushing to my face. Constricting my abdomen, touched with my right palm, tightening its wall, my chest held for an uncounted moment, my left arm limp as if it has been withered for a long time(I don't recall this injury)
Is there more than one past? Without one past, I cannot have a conclusion(but this is not true)my conclusions

and pasts are mine, all that is mine, if they are findable. Losing my iguana expansion, I become starving and(as if)emaciated again.

4.

I must follow happenstance, till I've run past(till I've collected many horizons)invoking the past so that it is no longer false(still not true)I will not worry about this any longer. Hearing lines of dust trickle, I am my mourning, begun my ascent, approaching disappearance in the blackness(the length of my existence)I lay my face away in my hands, climb another step, breathe slowly up this slope.

I am looking for my birth
rising from my birth
I am looking for it(I hear it behind)
I must remember my birth(a resurrection)
An Obsession.

Immortality is baseless. Unable to continue this walk without some untenable affair of blind faith, unable to reestablish by lines clean of untenable faith(this impossibility accepted)I continue its walk.

Where is my casket? I will walk to my death.

In my dream I am the door and the key and must find a way to fit myself into the keyhole, levitating before myself, waiting for the moment I will slip in. Laughing a nervous fit of laughter, I crawl onto the eighth step, out of sight from my sticks and my created time.

Please, please show me the door so that I can open it.

I am glad you finally believe—Kadman reminds me—But it isn't up to me. You are the door and the key. You said so yourself.

Kadman can now read my dreams.

How did you know? I was only dreaming! Stop penetrating me!

I can't or you wouldn't be speaking to me. How

should you understand yourself and yours if not through your dreams
your thoughts, your history? I
was waiting when you were pushed from her loins. You couldn't have done this alone.

I didn't ask for you. I didn't want such a soul. I will wash it from my system—Another abstraction
is the soul. A fool's paradise.
I walk, drawing a face of circles with my soles(a sign)counting now eight or nine, not sure of my count of steps, having lost count and starting again. A repetition of starting to count over and over again.
Hurry, before the wolf
Hurry, before the wolf sinks its teeth
Hurry, before the wolf sinks its teeth, devouring your aging and decaying flesh.

This is only a pose—Kadman says, shoes tapping in this sanctum—Where has your shaman gone?

Aren't you The Shaman?

I've seen The Shaman here before—A girl's finger pokes at my chest—The Shaman is here!—She looks to a sky, adding to my confusion. I play another tic-tac-toe, my X hanging apart, disconnected and useless

You are The Shaman of the modern day. I am just the peon, the one who moves in circles from birth unto death, the one who leads you when you are exhumed, that will converse when you're lost. Have you ever acted with your soul?—Kadman asks.

Is it necessary to be so sure? I have difficulty accepting less than absolute answers.

Then accept no answers. A pity. Your death will be a pity—I hear Kadman urinate(toward me?)
I have lost belief in my parents' parents and those before them and backward until...But what? But what of my

ancestors? I will not reach them as far as I go(is this what I have been trying?)Retreating further. But to where? I do not know this place
chasm of forebears.
I pray for myself. Only we have faith or are faithless. I have not found middle ground(is there none?)the negative energy choice(sounds like a soft drink, I remember, yes, I remember this commercial)anything to distract my sense of mortality until the last moments, whether they last a laugh, the smell of fish, tasting my own blood, or all of these during intercourse, or each one millisecond past another(or not even a millisecond)or dwelling on errors(for in the last moments we have nothing better to do then dwell)recurring indefinitely in circles and again.

No! I do not consider eternal recurrence! I do not want to pass through here again! Where is the true haven?—I ask no one specifically.

We can get you there—Says Kadman.
Trying to reach light to hoard, back in grayness(is the light still up there?)Time has covered my skin in dirt, changeable, blowing sand burying me, woken from I can't remember, another blotch of uncaught scenes. No longer entire, I must find my parts to survive. Covered in this sand, I am buried in the same night and the same day as was the last time I was here, and the times before that, led back to my first creation of this pyramid.

Wait!(is this true?)was I here before? Kadman, won't you answer me!—My voice breaks into a squeal and coughs, my veins oversized, swallowing my blood—Where will I begin?

You search for answers in your history.

Will I recall my birth? Will I be near timelessness when I know my birth as if it were yesterday?

You can't be near timelessness, but timefulness.

You search for answers in a history—Remember—
Kadman repeats—It is left to you to gain back a tradition.
You can never rid yourself of some necessary myths.
Which?

5.

I can be seen(so I believe)here on another stairwell in the grayness(I am not used to these eyes)so I climb higher(it is no longer safe with strangers staring into my trial)to find another overlook, but there is only another ledge. I kiss another stone, inhaling its aroma of soil and the air of this place. I throw it with all the strength I can find within myself onto the stairs above(with the others?)to hear it echo into an unlocking.
I imagine a seagull close and filthy, flying congruent circles, beyond my unseeable(or is there any?)ceiling?
I latch onto the seagull's rotations and traverse a great distance. In the sky I see colors and each one I remember redorangeyellowgreenblueindigoviolet.
Here the rainbow stops; I cannot regain intuition locked away in this place.
I repeat a physical definition because I am afraid of this place(the newly unearthed intruding my isolation)based on half digested information. I touch my adam's apple to feel each vibration of my chant.

There is no moon
the sound of a conch
urine and excrement
it is hot
6206514...but it is not like a cant.
I have found no God
gods
truths

(this I stop, hoping it shall pass for my life)

I have not found the light
Kadman is or was here

(and sees)

there is a pool of water somewhere that I can

hear

    there is a rumble when I put my ear to the floor
    I am finally unable to tell the difference between
imaginings and realities
(not finally, but now I must admit it)
    there is the caddisfly
    the cricket
    the fly
    the lightning bugs have gone

I look backwards(perhaps I can escape without movement)there is only the darkness, some wall in some direction(I am not sure which)smelling the mortar's dampness.

    Enough!
    Be rid of these things!
    Stop their noise!
    Uncover my grave!

Something must.

It seems I have just been rushing circularly in this darkness for many years. I feel gone, losing touch with the foottaps of my ancestors, no longer know where my feet are to land. Touching my testicles and listening to my heartbeat, I stand and try to remember my medial line but I cannot bring this off fluently, on the verge of fragmentation. I will have to crawl again. We are given the power to congeal our parts(we usually do not)I close my eyes and breathe

da dumdadu du dam du du du dam da dududu di di ddddd dudumdu at my

toes, I feel them tingle from their loss of blood dddd duda my breath following each fourth rooftap and each splash until my fingers tingle ddddudddduddddu a splash and it is like it has fallen onto my face(a moist mosquito lands on me and I am bitten and my muscle does not tighten

but I touch the spot it has left, gladdened by its landing)wet, my tongue glides across my lips. I will have to land. I stretch my arms before me like a sleep walker and count the steps I move.
onefoottwofootthreefootfourfootfivefootsixfootsevenfooteightfootninefoottenfoot
Counting my day by recounting steps as time. Foolishly trying to incur each detail, as if when I struggle hard enough, I will be sure I am recalling some unaltered fact, thinking that finding unalterable facts will lead me away from this place, but instead bringing me back to death as one of those facts(not proving this place is my death! There's the hope!)

You can leave now—I am told. A rectangle(the size of a coffin)above me, alight, ricocheting to me(I try to hide but am afraid to jump from the stairs)I hear pulling and unoiled hinges. Turning away, I am not ecstatic(what is wrong with me?)unsure if I should go back into the hole, looking for the unlit
again(it will hurt at first)to see or lose myself, unsure which I prefer, one so easy and the other an agony.

Oh God! This place stinks!—One of the strangers yells.
But I find I disagree.
I hear the hinges again, the flash of light gone(panic and relief at the same time)there are things I would not say(I would not do)in daylight.
I weep across the floor, rubbing my fingers together in the muck. Having listened in the darkness, halted in the darkness, found
things in its blackness. To hesitate at my escape(like a mole, I shy from the surface)In empty sunlight there are only two ways to exist, either create or decay, and most will fall into decay. Is this the pit I will rot in? A pit of

indecision and staleness.

You can't escape—Kadman says—It is not difficult for both of us.

What riddles do you play?

This is the way.

The repetitions, I've learned the repetitions by rote(in the repetitious chants is to be found energy that is necessary and extinguishing)

The repetition of work
of fornication
of generations
the repetition of establishments and institutions
of property
ownership
owned lands
of owned traditions
Not to jeopardize oneself for a stranger

(Is he or is he not?)

not to disbelieve in gods
the prayers
in oneself
not to do destruction only to oneself
not to commit suicide
in soul
and of continuing life as pure
the repetition of

Our instinctual desire to be free of
bodily pain and
And Yes

the repetition of our desire to be free of soulful pain
to gain these
the repetitions of hiding
of thinking on death

habitual thoughts and doings.

The repetitions of salvation—

Kadman. Don't you want to be saved?

A vulture spirals near my skull, on the wind encountering a downdraft. I push my knees against my ears, and hear it as if from my joints—Where can you go? What incense do you want? Is it mace?—It circles hawking—When is it your turn?

Aren't you starving, Adam?

And you?

I've lain here too long to starve.

I smell algae, a fish cove, a woman's roe, jump to follow it, but my arms cannot carry me aloft(I am)too weak from my beginning. Something follows(has been and will be)me(must run from it)giving birth to myself, our sperm(killing itself with the wrathfulness of its groin)Man. I cannot escape from Man's entanglements, my tongue licking my thin lips during the time this situation is recognized as necessary, the rain coming down harder dumdumdumdddumddddadumdadumd-dddumddudceaselessly

Even the insects have quieted, waiting for the storm
to pass
temporariness
temporariness of our security
our homes(our places)
the temporariness of families carrying vessels filled with their blood(impregnation)to be poured, soaked into the earth, discarded(the only things, death and their hope)the continued births(what is it I want but cannot find the words for?)the
Incommunicable.

Sticking any pebbles found into my pockets, I try to feel as if I own things. Without defined space, I cling to objects for importance or for a right to exist, to know I have gained something, to bring something out with me in case I forget again. The hinges cawl, the light increases and the pebbles have become my domain.

Look at him! Look at him! He will not come out!

A new voice? Who is that, Kadman?—I ask.

What?

Is that you?

No, but I will see you soon. We are here.

Slow in the morning—A voice repeats—Look at him, grasping the steps with his hands—This may be safer, knowing another sees the things I do(as if Kadman is not another)adding some finiteness here, others agreeing with what I see. A part of what is before me.

A footstep may or may not be of help in your life. It is important in what direction and what is stepped on—Kadman says from behind.

What is your name? Who are you?

Shekanna told us to look for you.

A precursor to birth these women speaking to me.

These are the stones of an oven—A second voice says.

I wonder how long he has been here?—A third voice quails.

Always must have been someplace—I say, feeling crowded although they are not upon me(yet)feeling the need for an excuse to continue—Let me pray for a moment—I clasp my hands and pray so the powers surrounding me can hear(perhaps they believe in prayer)

I am
I am a
I am a lamp
I am a lamprey eel

I repeat again and again, the prayer running through me

like ice water, a chant filling my limbs.

We better get someone to get him out—The third one says, but I continue to
pray.

And the incommunicable things?—Kadman says, forcing me to awaken a little bit further.

My soul?
Blindly following the possibilities of my rootings through night streets, not recognizing the houses surrounding me by my reflections. To avoid will change what is to come, as will to commit. As will to submit. Can I find the reason I am here? Is it close enough and far enough?

Wherever there is energy, an action will occur, even without attempt. The indifferent make a mistake—Kadman says, convincing me up another stair as the others from ahead increase their barter.

How's that?—One of the voices says—I can't hear you.
Choosing to affirm or deny, choosing from the patterns of which I am already aware.
Where are the patterns I do not know?

Remember this—They say in unison—It is not as if a choice is to be had—Unable to push their voices aside(attempting to gain some control in this hole)I rush toward them, up a number of steps, following another bisection to the west(hastening toward the light they came with)

The answer is not in hiding! Come out already!—The first voice yells.

I can swim from this. Don't go out of your way.
I start to chant for in chants is forgetfulness.

Thou shalt not love thyself
(to diversion)

Thou shalt recall

reconstruct
and recapitulate
(until one is clean of past and future)
as untimely as one can be
Thou shalt climb
(past the torii gates)
mere apparitions, shadows
Thou shalt be a witness
(of thyself)
of no one else
of habits and
assumptions and
We shall start with No
(addled addling adding)
until an affirmation
finally seeing with the memory
(of we)

Slipping into a well, will I fall too far and not return? I refuse to move further, holding fast to the stair, one of my hands searching for the ground to know the depth I must descend if I fall.

Did you find my social security card?

No, I didn't.

This is good. It has no use here and, if I escape, I'll get it replaced.

The tapping goes on, dum da dum da dumdadu dumdadu dadudadumdudumdumdudadum dddd I listen to the sound continuing and the splashing intermittently(I will eventually have to leave this)this I know.

—We need to grab it! We need to grab it!— Through my scrotum I can feel my testicles whine and twist, enveloped by their hands.

There! Now you're reflecting in the right direction—Kadman rejoices(his first unburdened happiness)

My chant exhales, their banter returns and increases, finding the beginning of my prayer(I try in vain to exclude them from my time)I want the energy to drain from me, like runoff during a heavy rain causing mud slides, my feet sinking and feeling the paste entangling me.
What gave life may drown me.

I am

I am a

I am a lamp

I am a lamprey eel

I will swim from this. Don't bother yourself...Yourselves—I am surprised to be conscious of my speaking, as if I am sure there is more than one. Looking for the cut on my knuckle(I lick my hand to feel its terrain)suckling for blood, planting for my power.

There won't be any progress if blood is not spilled—The third voice says.
(The swallowing of our own blood(a distortion of our power))Kadman attaches to me as a leach, forcing me to rise and climb still further, thinner air and twilight lifting. Quickly leaving the second bisection of this helix in the shadows, I can see it. Yes! Just beyond the peak. For this I stop, sitting head wrapped between my legs, all the mingled
voices coming down the stairs.

Whashrongitdoadadisemum—The voices say.
In search of the terrain, I close my eyes, picking up momentum until I am gliding past at highway speed, the guard rail and streaks of color straight ahead becoming a malaise. Alone(finally, I am sure of this)no distractions for moments, moments of silence, slipping from me wonderfully, sipping paradise.
Mother comes in and sits, breaking my cover.

You'll have to leave—Mother says.
She is here(has been here at all times)huddling into me like near exhaustion, shaking amongst the trees at night, having no home or direction after all these years of child rearing(my sustenance before her abandonment)
Son, come out to us—One of the voices says.

A Crooked Circumference

Too lazy to force it to rise—Kadman says—You let all your energies dwindle into me and this crypt. Now is your chance! Survive!
Spiraling like a rolldown stool spun forward fast, back to my beginning or till I lose control and am decapitated, each circumference a long way around, a repeated flight a gull airwise.
da d dudumdu du du da ddumdudumdum dadd du dddd du dum...splash...something has fallen(dddd)away. Eventually losing count of the rain, I reach for the future from my place here, searching for its dimensions. I will be rushed past each horizon, never able to see my times, only perchancing on fragments of past events, beginning a wandering through the desert of my time.

How do I know this? How do I know you will lead me out?—I ask my guide, but he has gone ahead—I'm here—I say—Here!—I find some peanut shells on the ground. Each shell crackling beneath my feet(a trail of sound)I follow him—Here!
This is the living here—I have become fearful of my aging and my recognizings(each recognition carries with it a movement toward death, a past event)swallowing saliva, shrinking like a slug retracting from a flame. I feel vague and odorous(the imposter of my head)a recurrent criminal returning from authorities, wanting to slip by

them.

Is this clay in my corner the remains of my maker?

Who?—Kadman whispered. Wispers.

Who is? Who is my ma-ker? My maker?—I can only despair how even to pronounce his name.

I was born beneath this roof, guarded from the rain at certain times. Flat, or triangular, it has never left me.

How are you so sure then?—Someone speaks to me(other than Kadman, the rain, or anybody I can recollect)—Mother said I was born in this—I answer(but to who?)I cannot remember this voice. Who? I...

It sits and weighs on you?—The second voice asks about what I don't recall being asked, to affirm a thing whose memories flew through me(in this way I forestall the last few steps)inexpressibly.

They call me again—C'mon, you don't have a long way to go this time—They cajole.

Creation and death(the voices are very close)they whine—Shall we pull him out kicking and screaming?

Kadman shares with me what I certainly did and did not want to become aware of—Your elliptical orbit is deteriorating quickly. You cannot circle too much longer. You'll fall into the atmosphere
and burst into flames. Prepare yourself.

Now you are addicted. Can't you see you are dying?—The voices say.

I toss this question aside with others, having lost their count and the rain.

Behind, no chance of food but my obsession to continue(for the first time I am glad I do not see, but only feel the space)Lost in my aging.

How can I save myself?

Escape by recapitulation and reinvention—

Kadman provides his first repetition(like upchucking after a drink, too much recanting)

Our battle shall be lost again—Kadman continues.

By whom?

By mortality(this is my first strength)

Must I survive?

You must make the answer—Kadman chimes—I must wait till you have the strength to be given more information—For the first time, I hear Kadman doesn't have the strength to reinvent alone(this I have denied before(an important assumption for my Kadman was a god)

Grab it! Grab it!—Their chorus whines.

Come with us

We are waiting

Grab it! Grab it!

you are addicted

and must go

come here, I have an injection for you

Grab it! Grab it!

Cabdlitrintranabkit—The three voices say.

Do not touch me! It grates on my nerves! Leave me be! Pour this into the dirt! Leave me be!—I try to remember when and how I ended up here, even if I can't recall the crimes that led to this(could it not be an action, but a thought?)

ddddudddiddyddidddudududududydydydydididid-ddddddddddum

dum d d d d d dum dm

But then who, Kadman? But who are you?—This question infects my mouth, creating a coldsore(here is a change)—You—I hear but having heard the answer, I do not believe.

I remember my last draught from the puddle, the dirt, rust and stand. Rising, I walk at first slowly and unsurely. Resisting on the next to last step of this first staircase, I cannot find the instance, that entrance, that began this(dadadddudum ddddddddddddadididydydadududady dydydydydum(t
t)dadudddadududadidedum)

One day we will leave here and I will bear children for you—Phoenix said.

Are you pregnant?

Singing, I try to recognize a face in the night(having become accustomed to this evolving dark. No longer thinking it will ever change to dawn, I look for the voices at the top, living things, this silent and deteriorating darkness, not as encompassing as before, images made of shades of gray on gray forming shadows evaporating. Following my guide, searching for his route, losing him(to where?)I touch another stair, turning round, but he isn't behind. I start from his last place, following his illusions, knowing his past.

One day we will leave here and I will bear children for you—Phoenix said.

Are you pregnant?

this child is me
I've admitted
(this thing finally)
I know the child.

Adam, wait for me!

Don't you want to get out?—The third voice says.

Returning to my child's babble, I see frogs. They've come when there are no cicadae and fireflies. I recall dissecting one, cutting a thin blue line across its smooth plastic screen, finding no blood flowing but frozen. His organs strewn, we wished to see his brain. Cracked skull, I saw

it, lime green and lapping.
Letting my pebbles drip through my fingers, I dream I am in a row boat with three women, their faces still hidden in their darkness and my inability(even the boat cannot be seen)Watching
the concentric rings grow further and further outward, I begin(from
the outermost circles)to recognize past sounds, a rattle and foot
stamping.

It is much easier—My Shaman responds—Then you think.

Leached of my blood. Leached!—I shout—Of my blood!—This is what I'm doing now; reestablishing links to before, in order to discover my place.

Circular, isn't it?—The Shaman laughs.

Another one of your tricks?

You are too easily fooled to need tricking—He coughs six consecutive coughs, dryly.

Where is Kadman?

Why, he is here. You've been speaking to him.
Muttering—Of course. Of course—I turn away.

By isolating yourself from your anatomy, you've taken leave of yourself—Kadman begins—You've turned yourself into bits of thought, only speaking to one part at a time. How are you today, said to your forehead. You are too cerebral, said to your nose. You do not want me, but an image of me, to your left ear—Some warm breath on the nape of my neck, I smack at Kadman, only striking my sticky skin.
Another unearthing of memory(buried our days)a recurring dream with sounds and smells and images that will remain as long as my language and species continue to exist, measurable by our biological time(for me this is

the only time
that is not tainted by past or future, but only sits in me unpredictably)

Flight from your flesh has been a major reason you've fallen from grace. You should stop idolizing images before yourself, learning to recognize yourself.
In another daydream Phoenix and I are lost in searching for sky through rain clouds, kneeling down then kissing the ground, not less portent than the head of our sperm each launched egg, our blood's power(but first I must find it)become languorous
in its lost and floating. I believe, when I have these illusions or dreams(I don't know which)I recall middles to beginnings, leading to middles, unreached destinations. I have yet to find an end to this dream, an infinite digression poured from the body, unforced but found, relentlessly needing the strength I can only come upon from prayer or chants praying thusly(running in a crouched attitude more and more hectically)a wave full of terrible strength, raised to moments of ecstasy(dissipation in a seamen's outcry)raising the spectre of my scourging. I try to clasp onto
the movement of my wind(everywhere
it is calm)Used, my energy builds bridges and creates thoroughfares for escapes and temporary niches, but doesn't find what is religiously
buried and incommunicable.

Where does my niche hide?
I strike my abdomen, seeking my core, finally vomit into this place from dizziness. I have given it my rank alcoholic juices, given it my sign.

That is why I can't get caught—Phoenix says from above—I am a ghost and an apparition.

Am I an apparition?—I am hoarse, speaking to

continue searching for answers, as if speaking aloud could somehow get me there.

You are not my shadow—She responds—I am leaving you again.

Drawn out, the light stabs my eyes, building me again. I must feel safe in this illusion.

Living so long without light, I've lost touch with the sun.

Have you been here for a long time, Adam?

What's this? I hear my name! How do they know my name?

How long is a long time?—I ask.

You must come out, my son—All three say—I am going—I am the abandoned one now, so I decide to abandon this place.

A butterfly, new to this world, alights on the door jamb.

Mourning death is remaining in this place—They stop and wait for me. Still incapable of not mourning, I squat just before the door jambs.

I

I am

I am a

I am a piece of me

I am a piece of meat.

(and I cry(two or three difficult tears(crying so difficult yet(because I wasn't even this just before.

We are all the same algae, from the same sea. No. No, don't wait any longer—The third voice says.

A seed of knowledge—The three voices remind.

Touching my scrotal sack, carousing my hands over my body, I feel its power, filling my abdominal wall, indefatigable.

Are you sure you're alright?—The second voice asks.

I am.

Yea, I bet. Don't let's stay here, or next time, we'll not be able to push you out—The first voice whispers.

Who are you?

To finalize your imprisonment—The third voice laughs without happiness.

Her hand reaches through the darkness—Even thoughts can be others—Here, this way—Other hands appear and gently raise me.

Uncoiling past the jambs, away from these haunts, I see the three.

How did you find your way in here anyway?—The second voice says.

Checking my face, saying—You're new—They stop me—Next time you're here you'll be taken to a less preferable place—I am surprised.

What is a more preferable place?

they laugh.

You must purify—They say.

Yes, but not just for myself—I stop.

Yes! Only in yourself can you reach such depth.

I can't hear myself. Not even my refusals are heard.

They come in blue, two, encircling, looking for me—Please—The voices say to them—He is not mad.

Putting one foot before the other, I look up at the sun and laugh with acceptance that nothing will change; I had not disappeared well. Pointed out in a mirror, I open my eyes and focus and look at myself, my face streaked in solid black-speckled stripes, my hair brown and matted and dry blood just beneath my nose(I cannot remember a nosebleed)but my eyes, yes

my eyes, they glint, they are full. Full. Do they know where to go?

Where the epics of my thread can be found?

Live well—I say, taking cautious baby steps, as others I can not place stand aside, deeper, finding me and losing me so many moments to so many moments. I see so many people sitting, people walking. I wait to mimic these, my species, again.

I am
I am a
I am a lamp
I am a lamprey eel.
I can swim from this.

The Sandbox

(a culture circling)
Catching sight of human forms
(from above waiting)walking
Composed of three(swooping down,
circling)Uncovered and nude
synchronized and brown
from mirage to mirage.

Forgotten how to land, I splash into the sand.

Flotsam murmurs, the direction of our drift jumbled with collusion. Sunlight rakes my eyes; I grope at my head. Scrambling to my knees, I look through the fingerslits of my hands. Children's heads peep and bob, spring back behind a shale wall. Cacophonous. I shut my fingers in a long wait, hide in the rest of my palms.
Now-you-see-me-now-you-don't.
A spittle of sand.

Eeeeaal! He came outta the hole. Spiders have caught flies in his hair!
The future, from this peek, splayed amongst them. I want to ask the shadows for things that are chosen(they murmuring something indistinct)Incoherent.
Jubilee walks across the sand, pulls at my sleeve and pinches her nose—Come'on. Come with me. You stink and need a shave—She touches my hand, observing its lines—Strange, your lifeline has been broken. Where is that part of your life?

What part do you mean?—I ask.

That part, I guess, just before you found us.

I touch my scrotum surreptitiously, cupping my breathing organ.

That isn't where that part of your life has gone.

I pat her flat red hair, tempted by the eighth-inch space between her two front teeth—It's been a long time since we've seen you, Stone—She pulls me along laughing—Come with me and enjoy the sunshine.

I wait for a repetition of the murmuring. Unable to cry and to sing(they will happen at the same time)I wonder about the time and can't find my watch.

Sheckanah gets up from a bench opposite the sandbox, approaches, her large hips shaking angrily.

What's the time?—I ask Sheckanah in the distance. She looks at me dismissively—You are not ready for the time. What reasons do you have for even caring about the time?

What's the time?—I yell past her to a hooded man sitting on the bench, but he speaks inaudibly. Asked for the repetition of his phrase, I hear an incoherence again.

I hope for a solution, look for something to do with my hands.

You are not ready for the time—She reaches the sand, passing the wall and eucalyptus trees, their stubs bearing tiny tentacles of leaves. The children follow her, a girl with auburn hair full and long to her buttocks bounding, a black caped boy with thick eyebrows and blue eyes pulls his way over the wall. Slender children's fingers peek from behind gaps in the wall.

It must be near noon!—I shout, looking down and trying to tell the time again. There are no shadows. Sheckanah and the children surround me.

Your mother had the power to give birth and this is what she produced?—Sheckanah says, waving her hand dismissively and pulling my hair—Come with us. We have your seeds.

Do we have to go?—I ask them, but they flit and buzz.

Come!
(Come here(inside
Come(with us(in
side(Come with
in us(Come
the power(I have
the power to give you
birth(in
side(your seeds are here
Come!—The children spin cacophonous.

On the bench, he rises and swells, looms nearer, flits and buzzes.

Stop this light!
Leave me!
Stop this noise!
Go! Go!—A blackened shroud lands on my sweating carcass, blowing into my eyes, through my nostrils and my ears as flies(changed from their human forms)to my eardrums and behind.

Leave me!
Stop this light!

Buzz.

Go! Go!
Give up this noise—They say.

But I can't. I begin to cross the sand.

Beginning a wandering through the desert of my time, attempts at explanations.

Breathless Sand

Each flick of my line toward an explanation.

That way! That way!—Sheckanah prods me with her fingertips, driving me on—We are taking you from your first mirage. We are taking you through your first dreams.

(no escape from their hands)

We are trying to lead you back to your roots—The man says.

If I don't want to go?

But this is what you've made us for—Sheckanah says.

In the initial haze of foregoing our dreams, before the haze becomes habit and forgotten, when they are most acute and painful, revolve around me, no break in the chain. Vaguely(my organs roiling)I remember his narrow jaw, almond eyes and thick bracken hair.

Who is he?

You haven't figured us out?—Sheckanah's arm passes through mine—You really only know of me, Adam. You're always so confused. Why is he still my lover? Why do you look like him?—Her eyes blink rapidly and her lips purse(her tongue suddenly creeps out and curls)Flickering her hand like a dying fish—You smell like high heaven. Jubilee—She claps—We need a man.

Is he a long lost relative?

Her tongue curls back.

Never lost and hardly known. You may have lice, my dear.

Like flies, both flit out of sight.

I look round wishing they would not go, only seeing them far away on a gentle slope surrounding a mound, one eyed, an artery reaching like a five-limbed tree from its ear to the center of its brain, pink and violet dried

muscle. My eyes sweep across the thing they have made, touching my head and tracing from my ear their tree. Its circulatory system unfinished, no brain, no life in my eyes, no speech from my throat, no expansion from my lungs.
Like a dog, looking on all sides, I make my way.
My metaphysicians sing.

We must build him up
within an inch of his life
his arteries and veins
orbiting his brain.

Painting objects with pointed bones, bits of sand drip red and violent patterns beneath my skin. Some red specks, like red ants, flicker steam, the heat sending shivers through the air. I rub my eyes, but it does not change the red stream. Sweat rolls onto the bridge of my nose.

What are you making?—I ask.
His arteries and veins
orbiting his brain.
A Mandala—Sheckanah says.
From the sand, God made Man.
and we will be buried in this.
Of the sand and back to the sand

Finished, they look to the design and me simultaneously for a reply
(their making of me caught in my throat)
I drop, spiraling down toward my head.

We can't let our creation die—Their fingers traverse me, arising and descending across my face, my eyes and mouth closing and gaping to avoid their pikes. Sheckanah snakes her forefingers into my ears as her lover fills my larynx so that I can breathe. Their fingers swirl along my chin and throat, down to my chest and around my spinal cord. At my groin, their nails encircle

my testicles and buttocks. Losing ballast, I want to scream but don't know who will hear.
almost ejaculating onto my thigh and calf
almost opened and emptied.

What is the time?—I ask.

It's almost the right time to begin—Sheckanah says.

Sequoia

My blood's trails intersperse, dark red, exposed. Formed into an empty pod, translucent and sequoia colored, I am newly born, dripping, cannot speak out or hear. My darkness cannot entirely be eased.
Jubilee, callous covered feet, skips toward us across a field of magnolia blossoms peering upward at the ends of bare brown branches. Lilac and hyacinth limbs loosely surround the grove, invading me when the wind blows in my direction like heavy syrup. Her hair pulses like a skirt above the packed earth.

This way, Essau!—She yells.

I'm tired—He runs to keep up with her—Of work.

You never—She breathes sallow—Work. Besides...lucky I got you...from prison—Her breath falls behind her words.

Prison might...better—He says, catching his breath. A magnolia flower whips Jubilee's face and crumbles—Hello Queen—Essau nods to her lover—I heard you had some use for me.

Yes. Take Adam. Give him a bath and massage—She throws up her shoulders and her large breasts bob—Jubilee, then get him home—Digging into the pockets of her summer dress, rounded by her breasts and belly—Here is the way—Taking her lover's arm, she walks away—I'm glad we're rid of his scent. Let's go home. Mercury is aligned with Mars and I've begun to bleed. We have nothing to fear. Besides, Adam hasn't recognized us, Dear—Leading him through the magnolia trees—We have to follow his revival.

I am Essau, look at my hands. Strong but very soft. We'll pull this smell off your back—He touches my shoulder and gently squeezes.

Along the road, he grabs Jubilee's waist and swings her down. She laughs as he tries to kiss her under the magnolias, white and pale purple petals waiving in the wind and on the ground beneath her head. Throwing dirt in his face, she kicks once at him. He waivers back, screaming.

Whore! Whore! Damn my eyes!

I'll curse you when I grow up and know enough!—She says as he falters, beginning to see again and clearing his eyes—Come'on Kadman.

I smell myself on a wind that blows against me, of urine and unwashed time, and realize, really not for the first time but like the first time, that I must stink. We all become accustomed to our smells. I refuse to understand how she made this mistake, though this is a direction to take, an answer to search for, an action. She drops my hand.

Who?

I'm Adam.

Get him to the bath. I'll meet you there—Turning to me—What is it you're thirsty for, Stone?

I am taken unaware, without answer.

Descending upon a whitewashed building, inverted arches marking its roof, with sky blue doors. An old Japanese

Wisteria's flattened bark twists just above them, blossoming a call for wasps. An old man stands outside, bearded and grizzled, scratching at the confluence of neck and chin.

Step inside, step inside. Cheap cheap bath.

A bird screeches a high pitched heat discontinuous and subito, flies past us entering.

He will cost—He scratches his coarse skin.

Haunches on my calves, I squat on the heels of my feet pressing onto the concrete floor, water vapor raining into liquid across me. Mens' genitals bounce, their forms becoming more and less dense with the water vapor's opacity, passing to and fro.

Bidrinkcoinkha?—The genitals ask.

Visions?

Sheckanah, my genitals bouncing between her legs(I wonder at how she claims my potentate)grows from my forehead in a bead of water before my eyes.

Yes—She says.

In the muss, I think some question is asked of me.

Boiling

In this water is boiled the soil, full of unpredictability and hallucinations. If you drink, there may be visions. Come. Drink.

Sheckanah strokes my penis between her legs. Her breasts awash upon the curvature of her belly.

A glass of black liquid toward my lips.

Come, drink the earth and hallucinate visions.

Raising it above my head(trying to escape, afraid of the burning I(let it drop onto my head(scream, grasp at it light sequoia and gray(my hands burnt red and blistering

Boiled(my
visions and
hallucinations if
you drink(Earth
full of its soil(Baptized
begin toppling down to
my head(Given
Boiling soil.

Bidrinkcoinkha?—A chorus, I don`t know whom, might be behind myself.

You are baptized, within this region of our flesh, preparing to emerge—Sheckanah says, pointing to my crotch.

Dissipating in the mists.

Putting my hands between my legs, I move around my organ, hold and feel the breathing of each testicle to detect change, pebbles displacing then rearranging without expectation of finding my phrase.

I hear a trickle of water somewhere close, open my eyes and see a man big and bulbous with Sheckanah's tits, am afraid of him and don't know why. Only part of the mist.

We shall cool-off in this room—Essau says, laying a towel upon a dry concrete table—Lay on your belly—He begins to push, reaching my coccyx and pressing my buttocks firmly within his fingers. Specks of white, blue and green tile flake away, the history of this place and those who built it.

Even the desert has not escaped the ravages of man—Essau says, sweeping his hand beyond the magnolia grove. The air from the lotus-carved lattice rushes into my body, reawakening me to my nakedness before the sun, as if the pattern of my draining is completed and now I will refill.

Where can I hear the desert? The strength of this

place.
I touch my genitals to be sure Sheckanah has not stolen them.

First Gate

The grove surrounds us, its lilacs throwing off scent, filling the light blue haze of the sky. I see structures and forms on the horizon, a group of habitations, the beige sand moving like waves. The square houses are whitewashed, the doors sky blue. I recollect this represents the sun and the sea.

The sun and sea—I recite.

Come, we must intwine. You must strip. It's been a long time without sunshine—Jubilee says through her prematurely aging teeth, pulls at my pants—I've brought you new clothes.

But I can't right here, in the grove.

What does it matter? Hide behind the magnolia trees. It's better than in the open sand. There, you won't be able to hide.

I look at the trees, their flowers collapsing, petals opening and separating, revealing the circular center, like weeping after their youth has been spent.

Chase me Essau. Tug and pull me to the ground. I'm sorry about before. I want you so much.

What do I do with my old clothes?—I ask.

Leave them in the grove. Come, we must become.

Behind a magnolia tree they kiss, longish, wet, giggling. She, with long hairless legs, brings me down inserted, my head resting in the confluence of her neck and shoulder(Essau unseen)I can feel the beginning of an urging.

I jerk from this ambiguity, finding myself on the floor, my new clothes soiled, an animal`s dung heaped to my right and some flies buzzing. A yellow jacket flickers by. Essau parts the branches, looks at me.

God! You've finally dressed. Let's try to get this done—Jubilee says, flapping her hand in imitation of Sheckanah, trying to learn dismissiveness.

Which way do we go?—I ask(hearing nothing from behind my ears)—Which way do we go?—Hoping something might still hear. A plump and hairless(seemingly harmless)stranger stops(so glad to be amongst the harmless)teeth yellowed and at acute angles away from her mouth.

Go? Where do you want to go?—She asks, smiling, her hair gray but glinting(painless and harmless)against the sun.

To that city.

Turning to Jubilee—Do you know the way?

I was trying to show him, but he keeps lulling. Jubilee hangs from my arm, knees bent, weight suspended(I cannot catch her)Essau takes my other arm. I begin to run, stumble, try to shake the two loose(still pulled on)Fixed on.

It has been a long time since you have felt the glow of our sun on your sack.

Pulled down, I shake
shake to let them loose.
Fixed on me like parasites.

Come(to the
houses(of
sunshine white wash and(and
sea(come(inside
me)and see the
sea sunshine(Come

dress(Emerge, be
ginning recit
ations(full of
your lullabies)—She sings, fleeing and supine, my sand beginning to blow away, decomposing(my head still incomplete)
A song so loud it is heard in my memory.
I flee up an unending street following a white wall on my left, white minutes upon white minutes before I hear some words coming from behind the wall.

Be gone! Be rid of me!—From somewhere in my house, Sheckanah's lover speaks.
Hoping for a detour(but this is the only road I unbury from my text)Behind.
I(yes I)try wishing.
I could return without them, could always have recovered without them. Ten paces backward before the first shouts—Disemboweled you are. Falling behind—His voice answers, not beginning as it should begin a sentence, never ending as it should end its sentences, but a continuing, as if this was just a part of a longer script—That's not the right way! That's wrong. Don't you even know where you go?
As far as I can know, these roads reach to the sky behind or the sky ahead. I flee further into my maze(at least now I can lose myself)

Stop!
I stop before the entrance of my maze.

So, you think you are strong enough?—Sheckanah's lover asks me, seems to question from behind my nasal cavity, from somewhere in my forehead, from behind my navel, his voice sounding as if we are in a closed jar, familiar. Looking for him, I cannot fix him even behind me(picking at my clothes)but he is deeper than this. I toy with tearing my clothes off violently, laughing because they are the only clothes I have and this stops me, refocusing on the sky ahead.

There ain't nothing that way—Jubilee says—This way—She points to a gate in a whitewashed wall, its wrought iron geranium leaves chipping green paint—We can get in through there—She says, counts and caresses my fingers, rocking against my frame(I breathe in
trying to make it stronger, a part of the story)my toes crawl about their spots
trying to grab hold(this is something)
We always try to hold.

How do you know my address?

Stone

The magnolia grove behind, two-story crooked rectangles surround me with their ambiguous blue apertures. Like eyes, cast their shadow onto me. The children sit around a dry fountain, having waited for us to get this far.

Come with me!

Play! Play!

Be it!

He's it!

Catch him! Catch him!

Then he's it!

And he's caught—Besmirchingly, as I am surrounded by their city.

You are it! You are it! Now you have to catch us! Now you have to catch us!

We'll hide and you must find us!

Sheckanah sits, her violet dress full of her red squat nip-

ples, the sun glinting from her white powderstrewn cleavage. Her clouds move ever so slowly westward in her transparent abdomen. She falls(the clouds and the earth leaving her)the sun suckled in my mouth, her warmth full of the future. Held beneath the armpit of Sephira, Mother(wanting to remain there unperturbed)I breathe her scent, the pores of my skin open and curious, her hairs caressing in a light breeze, like grains of sand in migrating dunes.
Blowing all day against my hollow teeth.
I breathe and feel my lungs empty then fill somewhere deep. Somewhere behind my navel, Sheckanah's lover comes, as if some sentences have past, sounding distorted from a depth, the womb suckling air—Take it! Take it! See if you can catch us!—I step backward, pushing away a bone-colored fragment darkened by pale browns, chipped from before my conception. Forced underneath my skin, its tip lodges in my throat. I try to exhume it by upchucking, but it lodges more deeply, tearing my esophagus.

Swallow your bone!—Sheckanah says dry and hot(my bones still moist with their soil)She has had it since the first birth(a theoretical thing, unlike death, the initiation and the end)Swallowing
I fall against the white wall of a house while she rubs her hands over me, touching me with the middle of her palms, hands outstretched from the top of my spine to its bottom(flourishing at my asscrack)plied.

Swallow! Swallow your soil. It contains all the particles of your timelessness, your living and dying—Her voice becomes tremulous, on the verge of a jumble of notes.

I think he needs some sustenance—Her lover says, his voice finally clear(from behind my ears it is

Kadman's voice)An exploding(my gums bleed)sitting blanched and watching the crevices of the bone, its dried marrow reminding me
I am alive
I will die
(covered in the faint strain of drying soil)
my marrow drying.

NanaNanaNa, you can't catch us!

Count till fifty—Someone says—And then you chase us.

I open my eyes and don't see Jubilee, but Essau surrounded by two other boys in stripped shirts and knee-high shorts with bulbous cheeks and yellowed teeth.

Where is Jubilee?

She is hiding—Essau says—After you find us, we can rest.

The children laugh and rush off, behind blue apertures, white wallcorners and down the central white lines of the speckled black tar road.

NanaNanaNa. You can't catch us. NanaNanaNa
Growing fainter and fainter.
Onetwothreefourfivesixseveneightnineteneleventwelvet hirteenfourteenfifteensixteen
Like a history, I cannot stop my addictions, trying to understand; I find I cannot, so I continue to count
eighteennineteentwentytwentyonetwentytwotwen-tythreetwentyfourtwentyfivetwentysix

Catch us! Catch us! we will soothe your thirst—Sheckanah says—We will cure your dissipation—My marrow sits in my stomach, old brown and dry, waiting to punish me. I imagine it edible, becoming too liquid too sweet and too full of its own dribbling grayness, drooling down my chin, the scent of rain forests, thickly rotting from many generations of life, food for the next born, my tallow.

We will continue your rotting(if you are too weak)

twentyeighttwentyninethirtythirtyonethirtytwothirtythreethirtyfourthirtyfivethirtysix

We will give you power or prove less than a sustenance(if you are too weak)

If I am too weak—Sticking my finger into my mouth, I try to feel the shape of my tongue, its unsmooth and slick bottom full of blood vessels, my advancing teeth, my palate hard with veins. Calcium and almost odorless.

Looking for the bone.

Almost tasteless it is held before me.

Someone searches through my pocket

You had stopped counting. I couldn't hear, so I came back—A child says

Where?

At thirtysix.

Oh. You hide and I'll finish now—I say and the child is gone too quickly to have been lost sight of.

thirtyseventhirtyeightthirtyninefortyfortyonefortytwofortythreefortyfourfortyfive

I jump at a sudden coldness(as if I were in water, the temperature changing as the underwater currents flow)touching the bottom of my spine(my tail still dry)looking for the reason behind me(for my progenitor)

Which way should I go?—I ask(hearing nothing from behind my ears)—Which way should I go?—I ask, hoping something might still hear.

A plump and seemingly harmless stranger stops(so glad to be amongst the harmless)teeth yellowed and at acute angles away from her mouth.

Go? Where do you want to go?—She asks, smiling, her hair gray and glinting(painless and harmless)against the sun.

To...I have to find the children. We are playing a game. Ringolivio—I wave my hand in a circle over all the whitewashed buildings in the sun shut against the sparkling tar streets.

I saw one running below, that way, and the rest must be someplace. How much time did you give them?

Fifty.

Oh, well then, they could be very far.

Catching A Shadow

The rains—The woman inspects her few teeth, sucking them in—You should find them very fast or you'll get soaked—Forcing loose hairs into her scarf, she smiles and continues to shelter.
At the fork in the road, I recall one of the boys went up the shadow covered alleyway, westward, at its end a wall embowed leading to a growing world of hiding places. Covered from the sun, I sniff at the air and feel in its gaining heaviness the coming rains. Eyes back into my skull, gathering aspirations in my forehead, cumulus clouds.

Your face!—Kadmon says.
orange circulatious pools, undersea spires.

What has my face done this time?

It lies! It lies! When will it finally tell you something true?
the rustling of a tree. A raven's moldering squall.

How would I recognize something I've never found?
The pressure of my eyes pull at my face, a small squirming dissipation.
Glimpsed.
Releasing my pressure my hold my hesitations resettling, the constant rain on my brain's other end awakening me

to the thought that I am somewhere in this confusion, my ongoing. I recall: The rains gave birth to you; this is what you can see; what you can believe; what your space and your insides are made of.
I Ascend the steep slope, touching the wall to feel for balance.
A tongueless guiding.

This is where you were conceived—From a tiny rectangular window, wet splutterings reach down in flat long droplets, growing dense as I crouch and rush. Misjudging, drops hit my head and darken the soil as a stranger waters her ivy.
At the end of the shadow, the intersecting buildings ajar just wide enough to slither through, my head slowly escaping
Looking for a shelter and childhood.
A brack mound, blacker than my head's penumbra, crouches. A freshly broken vine falls on my head, the moist smell of broken geranium stalks—Take it! Take it! Take your semen away from me!
The boy sneezes surprised, pikes my navel and dashes away. I breathe a large puddle of thirst trying not to fall behind.

We have your scent, your unwashed and your wriggling insides. We have all that is creative that you are capable, the passions you can only sometimes comprehend and then not entirely. Of your own flesh. Take it! Take it! Catch your flesh—My metaphysicians prevaricate, pushing at my rib cage

I've got you now, I've discovered your hiding place—I breathe in the rain behind my brain and the suffocation behind my nave. My fingers reach for the boy's cape, wrap about themselves, feel its polyester dryness, its unsnapping.

His cape's emptiness.

Breathe. That's right, breathe all the things we have given you slowly and don't rush. It will appear—
A voice somewhere in my head
remains emerge.
I unclench my hand, the rain forming a slight pool in my cupped palm. Each time I try, the water slips through my fingerslits, nothing within the lines of my grasp.

Still looking for your eyes?—I rub at these voices, trying to erase the direction—Here! Here! Here are your eyes. What use are they in this gift wrapped box?

NanaNanaNa, you can't catch me!
The boy remains in one spot perhaps thirty feet ahead, jumping back and forth, his tongue vibrating.

Lelelelelelelele...
Giving up some of the hopelessness of my deciphering, I run a little after him.

You must congeal them, in a great desperation, into a great
MAAWW!—My metaphysicians, apparitions say.

SlowPoke! SlowPoke! Thibbbbbbbzzz—His tongue wiggles.
In my small pauses for air, I can drink my broth. I begin to run a little after the boy, his black cape snapping through and fro in my hand.

Auilah

Adam Auilah

Adam Adam Stone. You must keep your part of the agreement—Sheckanah appears through a peephole.

What is the agreement in my name?
Continuing to lose track in my deciphering, I put a pebble in my mouth and salivate.

The agreement you made with us when you decided to be baptized and drink the sienna-colored waters in order to uncover you head—She gnats at my head—So your blood will flow and your container gain cohesion. You are here to confuse you. You're here to confront you—Growing accustomed to no answers or just enough possibilities to move on or their disintegration before my eyes.

Lelelelelelelele. Thibbbbbbbbzzz...

You want eggs this time of day!—Emerges from one of the many open windows. Approaching, I look through its decorative black iron rods and its cool blue window frame to see a short and voluptuous woman in a lily head scarf beside a yellow enamel chipped stove, her hands on her hips, staring at something beyond
my vision.
She slaps my face
as I pull back, the window doors shut cool blue.
The boy, laughing, I continue to chase, reaching to grab his twisting back.

The agreement to find your head, to find your text. Go on with its momentum, just enough of a possible answer to move on—Sheckanah bolts her hole.
My god(I flash)
Almost grabbing the boy's cape, my fingertips touch his border.
I remember looking for someplace, in darkness, walking through answerless.

Not again. I'll catch you—My breath giving way to catch the boy, babbling for my borders, following my sounds, like an ox smelling and following its master, stringing some meaning.

Where are the others?—I ask the boy in my hands. Heavy with my pebbles, I pick some out of my pocket and let them slip from my hand, their dust soaking into the earth—How should I know? We've scattered.

We go further into the city(becoming ever more deeply surrounded)to find my species again. I try to recall my entrance, but only remember flies entering my ears and a panic entering my head. I smell the lingering lilac and hyacinth, a sense of sprinkled manure. Walking westerly, toward a thick tangle of wisteria, yellow wasps hovering landing on open flowers, recalling my baptism in sienna-colored waters.

I remember my baptism. What's your name?

Amos. Your baptism won't help you here.

Looking at his bushy eyebrows and his clouded blue irises, I snap his cape round my neck.

Give me my cape!

No!—I dash to the left and the right, Amos jerking at it, back and forth.

It's mine! It's mine! Why do you want it?

So it can flap in the wind as I catch the others.

Maybe that will be enough preparation—I hear from a balcony murmuring, its occupants half in and half out of the shade, like a stranger you think you have known.

How am I to recognize—I can't remember all the faces I'm to find.

Who? Don't you remember them? You're so stupid. I'll go catch them myself—He dashes off
Capeless.

I hear a call some animal mewing in a desperation its last maw.

Running after the boy, I know I can catch him if I must for my legs are longer and I can be faster.

His feet kick at his ass as he runs.

Mawing

Why are you stooping?—Sheckanah asks.

Are you afraid of your animal sounds?—Her lover, Crown asks.

Go'on! Go'on! You can`t stop now—I whisper to myself.

Are you afraid of your own shadow?

Go'on!

I bet you can't step on your shadow's head—Amos screams from a distance.

(My skin tingles when their fingers
hairy as a black widow's
legs tightly rub against me.

Go! Go on!(Go
to your sounds(a
mawing
a cow mewing(G
O go(come with us to
this(mewing(your
mawing(your insides roiling
your maw—Sheckanah and her children, my metaphysicians, craw.

But if they are close enough to touch, why can`t they be seen? Waving my hands in a flurry, they are gone with my analyticity. A way to be rid of my apparitions. The sky spins an uneven spiral as my legs drop. Peering at the horizons and above, the sky surrounding me. I wish on it, praying to it.

Chuck! Chuck! Chuck! Up Chuck!

Amos looks closely at the rim of my nose.

My cape! My cape! Shit, you've ruined it! My cape!

A man emerges from inside a cafe, looks north and south

about the street.

Is he alright?

I get up and nod. In the cafe, people shift, offering unexplained rocking and canting.

Amos grabs my right arm to lift me—We should go in there.

What for?

I Think I saw Ambrosia.

Concentrating on the breath behind my forehead, I shake into something's call.

Unaccustomed to the space of prayers.

Ezi. Ezi—A woman mewls.

Prayers and lamentations murmur from the tables, some doven while turning their rings clockwisethencounter-clockewise. Some tap and look at their fingers. The glances steal across the room, stopping often at the western corner of the cafe.

His head. His head. We must find his head to bury him—Mawkishly mutter two mourners beneath their breath. TV images move silently above the bar, the sound turned off.

O'Lord God, forgive, I beseech thee, for how can Ezekiel see? He has no head.

A child's coffin is on a low black-covered table, surrounded by a pile of garlic, the men bowed and wearing white shirts, the women in black or brown breasttight dresses. A man sticks his hand in the space of Ezekiel's head.)My concentration too weak for my head.

O'Lord, I beseech thee, for how can we stand. We have no head and are so small?—A woman like a black egg with black lace hanging from her head bobs in her rhythm beside me.

Visionless. Visionless.

We have no head and are visionless. O Lord,

where is our sight?
Amos points to Ambrosia a faint giggling entangled in the mourner's legs, the forest green table cloths stained by tabacco, the smoke thickening. A woman unremittingly bobs before the garlic piled altar, two men on either side of her, one's big and weak coffee brown hand holding her with fat fingers. The other's eyes dart nervously between the coffin and the woman's maw. Each doven a cresting wave of marine splotched scum, another mewl from her lungs, water from which I gain more thirst. Musing, I walk and stand by the coffin, watching the space of his head for any movement. The man with the darting eyes takes silent note of everyone's movement.
Darting back to the woman's maw.

On draft? Sure. Here you are. Twofifty...

No, I can't put it on, there's a funeral going on...

You don't need to hear the numbers, you can see them...

You can't see them? Tell you what, I'll read the numbers out. Get your card ready; they're about to announce the winning numbers. A brew on the house if you win—Says the bartender, wiping a transparent glass dry.
The dead boy is dressed in a black tuxedo, cumberbund, a tasseled white shirt, and a red bow tie stiff and redolent of his head. Bending and peering between the mourners' legs—Ambrosia—I say to them—Excuse me, I have to get Ambrosia.

Where's Ezi's head?—She asks.
The men, all three, shrug their shoulders and touch their bow ties, feeling for their necks, lingering. Ambrosia giggles.

O Lord, We are too small to go on without some

visions.

Where is our head? O Lord?

Thirty-two, twenty-four...Sure. Here's another. Boy, death's a dry crowd. Ten, seven.

Let's go Ambrosia—I say, pulling her wrist and dragging her out, knocking over an empty chair.
Giggling.

Why does the girl laugh at our loss?—Asks the thick fingered man beside the mawkish woman beginning her mewling again as the chair hits the wooden floor, a faint shriek growing.

Ambrosia, why do you constantly giggle at this?

They're missing their heads. They're all missing their eyes. Just look at all these bow-ties below empty spaces!

I tug Ambrosia through the tables, between the mourners, Amos following with a handful of fruit, she tripping over their feet and knocking down more chairs.

Afraid I have become visionless, not recognized their headlessness.

Fifteen, Eightysix...Hey! Why don't you be careful with my chairs?...What? The last number. Oh, John, I didn't get it. You know, them throwing my chairs around...John, it's not so. Even if you had all the other numbers, it doesn't mean you would've won.

I catch glimpses of Sheckanah in the low sun, turning into a narrow stone walkway her ass like cumulus clouds, each cheek smeared with splotches of dark shape.

A birth mark, as if our uncleanliness.

Jumping up into my arms, Ambrosia shoves me off balance into the stream of people walking in the four directions of the juncture, too old and too heavy to be carried.

Don't you want to stop and play with me?—She

says from the ground I've dropped her to—Stop and play with me?—She wants.
Children clamor behind me as if waiting to ask a question, tugging at my shirt till its tail comes out.

Aren't you going to look for the others?—Amos asks.

How many more are there?

Five. GO on! The next one will make a sound when you find him.

Do you think this is the place to die?—Ambrosia asks.

Taking my eyes off the horizon, I try to meet her two black unreadable eyes—Was I dying? Was that what I was doing?—I try
to surmise
to continue my reclamations(of the unaccounted parcels of my head, a cant set generations past but still not lost)somewhere in my maw and mew, I am and our head can be found.
Around my toes, the memories cling
caught in the seed of my current
unable to stand on a ground.
My blood fixed.
The children play a game of It and I am It, running to find them, over wet cement and manure interspersed curbs. Not knowing what is the base, where I can touch a tree for rest. The vein in my neck pounds, children rush around me, giggling in recklessness.
Rushing through another alleyway, I slip against a light-drenched white walkway, my foot cut, a mound of red ants building(full of haste onto my toes)

Where is the tree?

Only in the shade we will let you cool. Where's our grave? Our head? We need to breathe again—my

Metaphysicians say.

I can't see!—Squeezing the wound so more ants will rage out
so I can leech out.

We are your Maws—Sheckanah says, a glimpse of light from her asscrack.

I would never lie to you—Reaches a voice with the smells of Basmati rice and meatloaf.

You lie—I say(inhaling)You lie—I say(the scent of food)

We can only lie if you let us—Kadman says, his voice in my throbbing temples and grinding teeth.

Be careful children. When he mews, he bites—My mother, Sephira says, her voice faintly coming toward me. I beat at my toe, the red ants now beginning to increase in panic(the children having run off)a passerby hurrying forward.

We will eat you alive until you are a shell—My mewing begins.

You have only to trust us, and it will clot and calm—Sephira says.

Leave me! Go! Go! Leave me! I throw stones on you! Lilliths and Jezebels!
The passerby asks the children to touch me.

Let me see your faces—I repent.
Sephira wraps my face in gauze. Breathing heavily and tiredly through the cotton swaddling, I say—I ask only for solitude—I say—Only for solitude.

Go! Go!
to your sounds, a
maw's breath.

(my hunger)

Mewing in your breadth
let go your

blood. Raid
of your blood—My metaphysicians mewl and remain.
I still have not clenched their faces
my Maws.

Mother
[Sephorim]

I beg my mother's name.
The cant's remains, cycle of her naming and reclamation.
Sephorim, Mothers.

Wait! Stop this noise!
Some foottaps break my rhythm a dissension in the crowd. They are babbling about something(they say it scarcely)I try to understand the need.

Stop passing by! Is Sephira dead? Where are my mother's remains?
Have I only imagined it?

We all must die—Ambrosia says, sitting between my knees.
From an open window, finches' sounds reach me(Amos coughs-up, something desperate caught in his throat)the cagebars' jingle. Ambrosia hums and my urge is to wipe my fingers through her frizzled hair. Hope for Yes. To the right a dark olive face with dense black twisting hair(yellow cowled)and black eyes look out. She sees me and rushes behind a peepinghole(My Sephira
life.

Sephira! Sephira! My mother is behind these walls!—I yell so the passersby will have to hear me. Snatching at the closed hold, I take a splinter, a thread-like black snake in my flesh which I trace losing sight of

it when it has gone deep—You! You're behind these doors! Open!—My breath becomes a shallow parting—Come out for me! Where was I before my mother gave birth to me?—Resting her head on my knee, I hold my face within the confluence of my hands, smell my palms full of entanglements and funk, a living under great heat, a dust and a semidesert surrounding as far as one might see. I recall a rocking to her hips, her breasts unrestricted and lactatious. Feeling Ambrosia's hair, bristly against my face, waiting for the moment she decides to strike, believing in the smell of her hay—I will let you into my intanglements—She says. I am pulled, beginning to feel my castration in her hold. I give up exit(in her doorway is the exit)lulled by her strength(my milk)deeply rooted(the
heat and the sun bathe me in my sweat)She is guncolored in the sun(occasionally remembering glimpses of a bright hallowed moon
full of the evening)I try to slip in and expand and exhume within her
heeding time
time
time to contemplate this intanglement.
Into the oral of her legs, interlocking locked.

Adam, cant with me and recombine yourself, revive yourself—I beg of myself in the oval of her legs.

The Birth
(an inchoation)

1.

I stretch back the overnight tautness of my face, focus on Ambrosia, a small chin the edge of a broad jawbone angling narrowly into small puffy lips.

Adam, what will you do for my belly?

The words said as a breath caresses the palms of my hands. My sensory nerves reach down my loin, follow my hands down her sagittal plane—I am becoming consumed by you—

I shiver.

Your head is reviving in spots—Before I can decide if this requires an answer, unable to imagine some answer, she retracts her belly

breathes deeply convex.

Let's go find the others and Ezi's head.

I must go about recalling where I have been because in these are the pieces of where I can go. All the words I have been will be all the words I can unmistakenly utter. All the dreams I can construct will be all the thoughts I can find.

I can't find

an inescapable path(Finding our way.

Only able to smell the palms of our hands.

What would you have without this?—She points to my forehead, touching a spot between my eyes(of cumulus clouds)A confusion driven through this windswept coalescing.

Come—She says—It shouldn't take too much longer to find the others.

And our heads?

Those are harder to find. They're all shards and scattered.

Unable to see the road just ahead, I hear shuffling, a plea to be found. I stare into a large dark hole(fast just audible smotherings emerging.

Ambrosia scratches my ass—You've sat in some bubblegum, Ugh!

Falling into my next step, my knee jerks and the darkness absorbs me, the slanting sun wanes.

You do not have sight, but the habit of sight. You couldn't see I was hiding in your shadow—Descends from a balcony.

I'm a combination of falterings.

Amos begins to throws stones into the hole waiting for the pain.

Ahh! Damn you bastards!—Twins rush from the hole.

You hit my arm!—The boy screams.

You're found!—Amos shouts.

Unfair—The female twin spits on the ground.

I must be able to see into my shadow—I whisper emphatically.

You can't(Look!
at the sun
a blind spot(ahead
bellyaching(to see
the edge(we
here mewling
underneath a stone and blinded
In your eyes
In your peelings

Look for me—Kadman's voice babbles from my shadow.

I begin at the past(always beginning in its sweltering)building the flickers of my present(an overreaching of the past)its lights a skipped beat scattered and quickly dissipated. My grip along its tip tenuous, time and myself straining at the juncture
to keep my footing. Eventually
constructing a part of my head, pasts gabbling.
Flickers falling toward a guess, tangled.
Watching Sheckanah's prodigous almond brown ass vibrate hurriedly past, I am immersed in her penumbrous shadow.

This can't be all, eventually all these heads must stick together for a reason—I say.

Because it comforts you to think so

because you make this so
because it comforts you, so you pick a conclusion—My metaphysicians say, their shadow cold. I remember we are comforted in believing there are reasons
so we make them.
Wondering at thinking and making reasoning.
I will eventually get to these
(my myths)

Once you have caught up with us, your senses and your thinking and your making. You will be dangerously rich—Sheckanah, Sephira and Kadman mumble inchoate.

How could I be so rich?

Construct a pattern of soul.

(My remains
Imaginings)

I have to recognize this, my inchoations—I am not ready—Kadman's voice repeats me at the end of his words.
Sheckanah's halfass swills ahead of me(I look to where

my penis should be)I recollect
she's had this
she's had this penis
she's had my penis, this sephira, my Sheckanah
our propagation.
(Kadman)my god
i flash
The beginning of a myth.

2.

I draw my breath back and feel, touching the space I once painted black. Is this how a womb feels? Waiting? Hollow?
I draw the circle with my forefinger around my abdominal wall, repeating the friction in the hope I will burn. The female twin spits, landing to my left. The male twin stares at his sister's spit as she turns what should be her eyes(a horizontal dark cleft)to watch my ritual.

A womb is a legacy my mother said. She says I'll be burdened with a child, just like she was me. Sometimes it is full, sometimes it just sits, she says. My mother says that I'll bleed soon, bleed my arid diluted smell—the female twin says.

Eventually, you will give birth, a responsibility of continuations—I say quietly, she having stopped, brunette and hair down to her coccyx and darkness in her cleft.

Na! I don't want no kid like me, forced to hide because of our eyes!

How do you see through the cracks?—I touch the cleft and remember I am just recalling how to see.

Discontinuations—The twins say, running away with their laughter—Someone's in your house. Let's go to see who's hiding—I think the circle again, imperfect as it should be and breathe in, feeling waitingness. Wait for the bleed but incapable of this kind of blood. Beginning to understand I will not know what it is I wait for until we collide.

Where are you again?—Ambrosia says when we reach my cylindrical building. The chocolate brown stairs creak as we go. Ambrosia touches my buttocks, smiling her offwhite teeth and withdrawing her hands

when I look(so, I try not to)
Following her buttocks' caress upward.
A dirty brown waterbug scurries large and quickly out of sight.
Ambrosia's hips sway and her nipples stark, remembering I have not rustled my hands over a woman's ribs and breasts in a long time. She stops at two because I watch her, runs her tongue along her lips selfconsciously. Three Trees-Of-Heaven compete in a small square of earth between this and the next building(a four-story tunnel)Branches passing through one open window, attempting to reach the promised light where they can begin to bear fruit. The florescent lights turn our fingernails pale purplish and the white linoleum floors pale yellowish. On the next landing, I hear the peephole click(an eye must blink)another neighbor hovers behind the door.

You must find your power—Kadman mutters into my thinking, speaking from the circle I have drawn. I want the seeds that I saw when my melon was cracked, spilling.
Sheckanah bounces past me on the stairs, her arms chicken's wings' flopping, her legs bowed and flapping. A large breadth of belly just above her groin striated beneath oily glistening pubic hairs, her large tits' vibrations originating internally
serous in their breathing.
A fruit bearing woman(I find her lusty)
one great myth.
Must guard against the assumption there is one great reason any one cause.
In the interstice of Ambrosia's legs, I feel the rhythms of my scrotal sack emerge, squeezing her hard bonny buttocks, the cleft of her chest inhaling and exhaling as my

chin pushes against her left temple, strands of her hair crossing my lips.

Not so fast. Slower, Slower.. .

I listen against her small breast plate her sounds.

Is it in yet?

Intent on her uterus.

Slowly. Slowly—She winces—I never thought it would hurt. NO one warned me 'bout the pain.

Breathing against Ambrosia's neck, her noise enveloped by my chest.

Yes, slowly. I can barely take it all in—She quickly gasps—Not all the way! Where the hell'ya going anyway!—The door unlocked.

In the center of my circular room, Ambrosia on my chief's-head blanket, a waterbug crackling beneath us. I breathe in and push hard.

Like mules you fuck! Like mules you fuck!

Ambrosia gasps my balls, cuming and pulling, a swagged dive.

To our uterus, only to our uterus—I mutter—My...(man)

Eehhaauu! Eehhaauu!

The children enter, dance around us, their left feet thumping then their right, a swinging dance(Sheckanah's ass swiggers)

Eehhaauu! Eehhaauu!

Like a mule you fuck! Like a mule, this uterus is of no use to you!

Eehhaauu! Eehhaauu!

Pushing upon the indian-chief's head one last jingling to reach her.

They swinge and thump together round us.

Eehhaauu! Eehhaauu!

The circle broken. Ambrosia rushes out into the brown

flickering hallway, down the steps in a flailing.

—I was just about to...

I was just about to...

Exserted.

3.

My geraniums brown and yellow from too little water. Occasionally, through the open window, a breeze lithely and insufficiently grazes my chest, the smell of hot asphalt. An engine drives away in some distance. I sweat in the morning sunlight.

My blanket is ruined.

Sheckanna sits on my red velvet sofa bed, stuffing scattered over the beige floor. She swishes her backhand, too lazy to bend toward me, too far to strike.

Nothing a little bleach can't wipe away. Your scum is not so permanent. Do you know the way?

You haven't told me. I don't know where and I can't keep moving if I don't know where. I'm tired and my toe hurts. Pounds. I either have forgotten the direction or perhaps I just can't say it.

Can't find the pieces of your head?

I am farther from my head the further I go. I'm hungry.

The smell of fetid vegetables exhale from the tiny fridge, some strawberries splotched in a thick fur.

Where is everybody? The children were dancing and thumping—touching my gender in remembrance—Humping. And then, in an instant, they're gone.

Jubilee will return pretty soon. I think you had better disappear for awhile.

Why?—Some vegetables siltifying.

Sheckanah pitters—The police will come. She's told.

She leans out the window, her palms braced on the sill, a high pitched whistling dying in a slowly descending drown. Her flower dress upon her sweaty creases. I think just one large nudge.

Why? What did I do, or didn't do, that I need to go?—My ice-cubes dusty.

It's statutory rape. You rapped one of your myths. You should've waited till you had some meaning. Some significant lies—Sheckanah descends from the window and lays down, her back on the Indian-Chief, my stain disappearing beneath her ass. Allows her legs to drop in opposite directions, the pads of her feet meeting, housecoat raised above her pubis.

Where have all the children gone?—I say, my hand touching her space, dank and fibrous.

Back in the shadows of your head. You raped a piece of your head, eschewed your finding.
Spit it out in disregard—
Her iris slips between my fingers, Sheckanah moaning a low groveling, my left hand's fingers in her mouth, her tongue pittering. A siren raises its clamor, her jaws attempt to close.

—Ahhh! Ahhh! My fingers! You bit my fingers!
(Go! Go!
Eehhaauu! Eehhaauu!
(Go! Go!
You can't enter
our uterus(exhumed
with a breathing
(our irises
blinked wondering
you were born(just a shadow for a head
a shell of Man—my metaphysicians say, surrounding, cowled.

The police are coming. Our nub must survive. We've packed—Jubilee hands me a small leather satchel—Some things for your departure.
I wonder when did she know?
She takes my hand, presses it—Come along.

Did you Know?—I ask her.

Know what?

Her lover's name and when I would have to go.

Neither. He calls himself Shuckles C. Mollusk on the street. No one uses his real name, except Sheckanah. It's been forgotten—Jubilee says, squeezing my thigh very near my mooring.

What's the C for?

Crown, because he crowns the Queen!—Jubilee laughs—But I know you've been crooning too. Ambrosia's told everyone all about it.

Hurry. Hurry. The sirens are louder—Jubilee pulls me—The police are coming—We run down the brown staircase
Sheckanah(still on the head of my chief)emits
a moaning, a highpitched grinding(so I can hear what she sounds like)making love to her lover(Kadman riding her above the stain of my sperm.

I forgot!—I stop, realizing—My tefillin.

We don't have time! Listen to the sirens! They're almost here!

But my tefillin!

We don't have time! Maybe The Queen packed it!—Jubilee opens the doorway, igniting the florescently lit hallway, the brown walls soaking up the sun preemptively.
I want to reestablish a prayer.

We must go. You can always replace it—She stands behind the light, vague and enchanted, amorphous
and dissipating—Just ask the passersby.

For a prayer? Who are you?

I'm one of your metaphysicians.

What do you do?

I lie and help you understand.

In lying?

No, in our constructions. We find the truth in what could be lies.

Jubilee lets go the door, the sunlight blocked, the florescent lights flickering undulating browns, my eyes blinkering as if I am going blind. Remembering all my places, hearing them, smelling them, tasting them and touching them, does not seem to make me breathe them.

You should try to do more than just collect sensations—Sheckanah says to me as if she knows my conversation. As if she's here. I look up the steps, but the fluttering creates too many undulating folds for me to be sure where she is.

I didn't know I still just collected things—I say, but no one answers—Did you pack it?

A long sigh passes originating in the faltering florescence.

Yes, Go on. Do anything you want with yourself. We can't stop your tongue from wagging. But go! Or the police will catch you.

It might be an hallucination or a dream, or something(I believe I can recover)Hearing myself drone a combination of voices, a confusion echoing from it. I open the door, the sunlight stabilizing the shadows in my head. Drawn tight against the brick wall, I spin down toward my head shrinking. The police screech to a halt(I tighten the grip on my bag)stepping in shiny patent leather shoes.

We heard there was a disturbance, some man humping his floor or something. Have you heard anything about it?

Yes—I say—Upstairs, on the top—But I don't look up.

Do you live here?

No. Not I—I lie.

FLEEING EDGES

The Faces of my Maws
(searching for sepharim)

Almost always falling, my body's angle acute, its pads and toes unable to grip, declining toward a cleavage, my faltering line.
Not allowing myself to stop.
Sephira waves to me from a ginkgo grove. She bends from her motherhood, hips emphasizing her din as they rock, my assignation.
A lonelytree hangs dispassionately
bark burned away and its mottled white and black flesh shimmery. I lean against its decadent bone, a crowd of people creating a panoply of shadows in the declining sun.
Meanderings walking densely.
Trying to consider their pattern and find a breach. A man with thick fingers and scars on his palms slices across my ambiguous and narrow vision, the bowels of our lives encrusted in his skin. I try to grab some of his dust. Through my fingers rush their soil and brittleness.
Approaching unintentionally my diffusion, the shadows move in circuitous speech rearranging without cognizance toward an aim, as if every one of these impermanent relationships are intersecting on the dried tanned earth, heaving waiverings.
They interweave and their glances(their eyes only occasionally look)are intent on passing
as if

as if they move to avoid stepping
move to avoid stepping near me.
Surrounded by a circular grove of ginkgo, I search for a piece of the answer in the pattern of branches radiating outward from the still living trunks covered in a thick hair of broad skirtleaves. Sephira's buttocks cut across my view, flying and lugubrious at the junction of her thigh, a bleary land on the verge of collapse.
Within her bloat her joints narrow and desiccate(With each footfall)
A scar begins upon her iliac crest, crosses like white canvas stretched toward her coccyx, dissipates. I try and speak with her passing head, believing she will give something to me, but her thin and frecklevined hand waves as if it doesn't understand. Just conscious that it was wanted. The passersby do not let me get close(my toe hurts beneath its bandages)my hands remain empty.
I must go. I must continue.
Not here, not here at all.
I try to get attention by clicking my camera in anyone's direction. Who will be the first to wonder why, begin a dialogue? Who? Hello? So bloated with ifs, still unable to find a single way
as if the air were ifs.
Sitting on ginkgo leaves, I lay my head in my hands and mewl, not for those who died, it doesn't matter, but for the passersby.
It doesn't matter.
Mawkish for myself in this space
Unable to comprehend who I am.
Adam Auilah.
(and me?)
I am Adam and I am Kadman.
And you?

I ask one passerby, pocked cheeks and his forehead covered in round tight protuberances.
In the dark(I finally understand this)Kadman and these pustules were always me. If a passerby stops, he might understand(the faces of the passersby the faces of my past)if he or she or any other would stop, I would know if I could understand.

Excuse me.

Wait.

Do I want your picture taken? Protuberances and all?

I raise my camera to shoot, but he turns his back and waves me off. None of them bursting, my pathology still adhering.

So, you still have not escaped the claws of your past, your habits?—I talk to myself, my condensed volume increasing.

Locked in a jar.

I do not answer myself(how shall I even try?)Wary.

The tricks of interior voices.

A picture?—My jar booms.

Picture of what?—Another passerby.

A picture of my terrain. Uneasy from the cliff, another mewl edges me close.

My scream is somewhere in this city!—I screech at another passerby, pale skin sweating underneath the sun. He seems to hesitate, takes a more circuitous route, covers his face with a newspaper in passing. Not one stops. I lay supine, the leaves rumoring in the windless afternoon, feeling the dry earth amongst my fingers. Turning into dust. Moved by the crowd toward its greatest density, I attempt to force myself out of their snatch, feel their breathing between my shoulder blades.

Sephira is suddenly sitting at some bench near the park's

edge. She removes her widebrimmed straw hat(no hair my God no hair)The top of her head flat. I look at her placid pendulous breasts and the knowledge that her genitalia is just from without my view(covered)because I am ambivalent for it.

No. No.

Fill me—Her eyes empty and look past me—Can you fill me?

I pry for the direction I came(or an approximation)to twist out of the street's pull, trying to leave her nearly extended genitalia falling away in the horizon, remembering the details of her rounded belly.

Fill me.

I cannot push through the crowd to sever the dialogue(only drawn deeper)Forced westward by their bantering. Waiting for her genitals littering before my visual space.

Smell, smelling the air full of bodies, soil, shit and faint grass cuttings.

Her eyes all I am capable of seeing, their darkness preceding like unlit space.

Sparrows call precipitously. Watching them struggle against larger pigeons for bits of food, the sun falling in squares geometrically covering the ground, the sparrows' whistles reaching a shiver upwards from my spine.

I open my fist like a pigeon's eyeblink. She is already no longer in the park.

You didn't fill our eyes. We need to begin filling our eyes. We are not empty, but our eyes are not full—She said before she had left. I carefully touch my closed lids(afraid I will poke one out)I remember the relief of my mother`s milk(or a vague fullness after a drink)Lulling visionless dream. It is the same.

I do not worry I may be wrong.

It is the same.

Circles
(parts of the same)

Is that right?—Shuckles accuses—Then there would be no reason for you to survive. There would be no matter for you to apprehend. Acephalous?—He laughs and grabs my shoulder in a familiar ping—You reformulate your head—He picks his nose in thought, holding the infant's head.

The mind?—I plead.

A few nerve cells at least. You need a paradigm is all—Handing me the infant's head—This was you before. Continuations.

Before?

Before you needed so many answers, a definitive who you are. Who you might be.
Some incompletion of a head.
Entering the children's playground, Shuckles faces the acephalous body toward empty swings and a few children playing in a sandbox.

Where does Sephira live?

I don't know her address. She meets all of us in playgrounds. Pulling my arm—Come. Go and swing.

Will she come?

She'll emerge when you swing high enough to see past the horizon line, no sooner.
I will have to continue on.
Coalescing
the baby's body jerks, its mouth opening soundlessly
as the day I was born, coming up for air to discover a terrain.

Stop! Stop!

Why stop?—Shuckles asks—Get on the swing.

To where?

He points—We can recover—I mutter.
Pulls at my sleeve—We can recover—He mutters.
I think when was the last time I swang.
My lovers, Sepharim, still hold me in their legs, crossed and tightening, my body
prying uselessly(death is with them)
We swing.

You can stand on it and pump your legs. Just bend your knees and tighten you thighs. You'll get the rhythm—from the swingperch, above the density of the playground, I see Sephira. Pulling forward, faltering at another apex, the swingbottom losing touch with my feet for seconds. Pumping my legs and my body in the rhythmical motion of my arc(Awoken to my open mouth and breathing)Wondering how high is the sky.

Don't go too high, you might get hurt!

Rising above the walls, Sephira now a glimpse in the horizon, my pendulum in its upward momentum, the glare of the sun(now before me)a slackening chain. Memorizing my thin blood and effusion
Collusions.

I can see her! I can just about!—I yell to him, turning to glance at her, losing the swingperch.

Be careful at the edges, you might fail!

You shouldn't scream—Jubilee's voice descends on the swing passing behind me—As the wind passes through your veins—I release the chain to seize her throat.
Death and our living in symbols is the need for mythologizing(
returning to it)as an abyss
running to the abyss(
hanging on its edge(
Where is my Kadman?

Bits of shard in the wind answering.
My body parallel with the ground than just a whistle of air unattached.
Grabbing for the edge
any edge
my flight
failing.
Jubilee swings past, a vague outline in my head.
The infant's surprised face lays against its ear on the green painted bench. Hitting the rubber matted cement, my breath stopped in midact.

I told you to be careful of the edge!—Shuckles says—You might get lost.
Lost means what?
The impact knocked the wind from my veins, compressed my organs.

The wind filling your veins—Jubilee's voice modulates low and high with her pendulous motion. I try to rise immediately, my head's precarious bobbling unable to breathe(killing me with air in my veins)I look at the infant head, her complete face still scattered in the surprise of my fall
as if her head can hear me.

AAAAAAAAWWWWWWWWW!

AAAAAAAWWWWWWWW!—I try to breath in its scattered face.
I begin to asphyxiate, a momentary recognition of my mortality(a drowning)counting the length and frequency of my attempts to breathe, Shuckles holds my arm upward.

Calm down. Lay back. You still can breathe. It was just a bit rarefied for you.
The skin and meat of human forms have been doing this for a time further back than I can imagine. Rush pound

and sweat.
An emulation
A competition
A growing pathology
A belief we created our eternities and time.

AAAAAAAAAWWWWWWW!

A momentary flash from somewhere so deep within that only momentary flashes can be perceived. An intuition, people huddling together.

I awwwww thawwwww!

Shuckles places his hands on my collar bone and shoulder blade.

Iaww Brawth—I bleat.

My blood still beats too short and uncontrollably. The child's body holds on to Shuckle's hand.
Having tried to attempt mythologies, tried to recall if I am repeating my germ.

AAAAAAAAAAAAWWWWWWWWWWWW!

My mind tired from its sense of submission, stares at Shuckle's yellowing teeth and ruddled skin.

What a toil.

He laughs as I slowly get up, still holding my collar bone and my shoulder blade.

Tell me where you must go.

I have no place to go. I am so tired and just want to rest—I say.

Shuckles shuffles with the infant's head to another bench, facing it toward me. Mimicking a crooked man, he sits and begins molding its face, finishing its eye sockets.

What reason can you give to believe the edges are more than a fiction? Do you really have enough?— Shuckles asks.

Molds.
Puffy and streaked with its suppuratious juices, eyes

squeezed tight against the white sun to come(my infant's head)Unsure what can be asked for, my stomach clenching for what he will say(afraid to reopen my eyes)lest he and his figure remain.
Lest they stay.
My fear is the same.
It is all the same.

How can I become?

Counting no answers, I only feel my heart's vibrations, a thumping, carousing blood.

Such a slow cohesion—Shuckles thinks aloud.

I will begin aloud.

We human beings live by some artifice—He hesitates, an empty spot, the sun warming my skin—Hairless and complicated, given the power of the brain for nothing but artifices. Here are your eyes. What can they see? What can they find? Put them on!—He suspends the infant's head toward me.

Waiting, glimpsing at the edge I try to balance upon, the swing still lightly twisting in the air, its movements incomplete. Jubilee beside me.

You had quiet a fall—A woman at the gate says—Do you know Sephira? Not all glimpses are parts of wholes—She says—You might not understand.

Feeling I am mistaken, her words bounce quickly off my head, unsure what she could mean.

You said you felt like the air was rushing through your veins, then you fell—Jubilee takes my arm and pulls me along, returned to guide me.

A hunt of playfulness too surprising.

Let's go to the Market—She says.

My bag. My bag.

Somewhere, there is still my sight, I know, surrounding me.

The Market

Tiny black flies circle bananas. I see pale brown eggs beside fatstreaked meat; beige, gold and red powders in corkcovered glass at the far end of the mall. Against a redbrick wall, men drink green stems and leaves immersed in steaming water.

An iguana on a leash before a flower stall waits preverentially for twilight at the end of its thong.

Beside the meat stall, water diluted blood drips, flower petals stained brown and curly white litter the ground, plastic buckets full of sunflowers, daisies, and yellow mums. An old aloe vera plant in an earthenware pot seems to climb the dividing wall between two stalls, its limbs an arthritically cupped hand. My feet rest on chipped and mossy stones while a radio plays a scattering of insulated rhythms and static. The scent of mint saffron and muscle fills my expanding head, caressing my skin with a kiwi's fuzziness; my breathing comes unhinged.

Uncoordinated, my solar plexus begins to ache. Searching through my bag, I find my small velvet pouch of prayer.

Unsure how to grab this and feed cleanly.

Eat something while I'm gone—Jubilee goes.

Will you always produce the skeptical or contradictory as an escape?—Shuckles asks as I peel off a kiwi's thin brown skin, my crate creaking—What do'ya say?

I mean your dilemma. You've brought us into your dilemma. Will skepticism and contradictions always keep you from believing?

The Kiwi's green seeded flesh(between forefinger and thumb)melting in my hand's closure. Its juices dripping down my fingers toward my wrist, translucent nascent juice.

It saves me.

You mean spare. This can't save. You are mistaken.

Right or wrong, mistaken or correct, it's the same here.

Here?

Here in what I conceive I recoil.
My words count like incantations
very thin, slithering in my throat
like a small bird's featherless chest(balding)

Eventually it's all a story. A good hustler has faith in their story, believes in what they're about. You were one of our most promising students—Shuckles says.

Until I thought there must be something better than hustling.

An abyssal plain I was offered, I have found. Unsure who has done the offering, not precluding myself(always preoccupied in catching myself(as if I'm not where I sit)I listen to my babble, my stomach grumbling for more and a string of saliva drips down my chin to tell me I am alive. Dusk lingers transiently.

I believe in death.

So what

Shuckles puts the infant's head in the stroller beside its lap and faces the carriage where the sun used to be. The grocery shoppers haggle and look, picking up slices of meat or fishsteaks and picking away foul lettuce leaves.

I bear witness to my mortality.

This is something different but of no great consequence.

I believe in births. Looking for another route, fishing for some words for recognition of my place in this hierarchy

to help me understand my role, my relationship within my world. Looking at Shuckles, I try to flick a mosquito from his forehead, but he skitters.
I will repeat nonce and nonce again and again until I have some statement, some affirmation(a belief as far as we can keep it)but where does one start to believe?

I believe you must find a shelter for the night—Shuckles rises leaving—Jubilee knows of a tinroof wreck somewhere closeby.
I lean against a wall, the crate creaking and awry, my legs planted firmly beside tomatoes, people haggling over this moment.

Ten tomatoes for a Cherub, two for a Throne.

Not good enough. I should get fifteen for the fat Cherubs I've got.

No can do. You just have to sit and wait for them to fly into your traps. They're not worth as much as they used to be. I have to grow these.

I beg your pardon. I've got a Cherub-coop. I raise my angels. I'll take the whole basket for two Cherubs and three Thrones, if he can deliver.
She flicks her hand at me, the vegetableman sucking his lip.

Where do you live lady?—Jubilee asks.

Ten Ravensneck street off Declension.

We're going that way—Searching through my bag for my toothbrush, my mouth rank and carrious.

What are you looking for?

I want to brush my teeth.

Have an apple instead.
A sliver catches between two teeth, forcing blood into my tart saliva, its meat tender and white. I hear the noise of the crowd falling to earth, smacking this place, its damp stones babbling. Somewhere Ambrosia passes, an orange

sun in a small part of another horizon falling away.
A parcel sits beside me where Shuckles was. Catching glimpses of lines written on its face, a jumble, some new language or code I don't understand. I peel it, the crumpling of its skin intermingling with an upsidedown chicken's quaking. Inside, images of my mothers, all made of chocolate, a card spread across their navels, reading `Sephorim`. Reaching in, I behead them, chewing each chocolate head, the juices melting over my tongue before flowing into my canals, my headless Seraphim.

I remember you. Knew we were close, felt your warmth. Now you are gone. So it all does not matter anymore—I tell the chocolate figures laying on the box's bottom—I am not responsible for anything.
I mutter my name silently
swallow my mothers' heads.
I look back into the deepening box, now too deep, as if I will be unable to touch or reach the chocolate bodies
their heads returning
nine heedless bleedings
their chocolate melting and cherry juice smeared on my licked fingertips.

Wake up! Wake up! Get up and go on. It's late and you have to go deliver the tomatoes!—The vegetableman yells.
I lose balance(the box heaving and waivering)just as Sephiras' hands grab me. I can't recall if my eyes were open as she pulled me from my box.

It's time to move on.
The market is closing. Looking at my shirt, I forget how the red stain became. I look for a wound, but find none.

Let's go down Declension, there's an abandoned shell at the end of the road. It's time to move on—Jubilee slips into the settling darkness.

The vegetableman gives me the basket of tomatoes. Touched, they are pregnant and
almost breathe, covered in taut skin.

You'd better not drop them. If they're not delivered, you'll be found.

A mosquito lands on my arm, bites.

The passersby crisscross in a web of paths around me from an unknown source, my space shrinking(surrounded)more and more people turning over meats and squeezing vegetables, looking for signs of decay. Their sweat intermingling in my scent(trying to breath them in)Ambrosia passes somewhere; I smell her perfume, but cannot see her. The vegetableman provides me a bag of incipient rotting vegetables to pay for my labor. Smelling my vegetables.

Dates? Pitted dates?

Another bag sold to another squat and broad figure in a filthy dress, omissions and bloodshot eyes surrounded by shadow. A mosquito is almost drawn into my nose.

The yellow jackets get thicker.

Dates?—He asks—A bagful of pitted dates?

Raising a wrinkled pitted oval, stopping before he releases it, watching something I have been doing. Motionless, I wait and search for my articulation. He drops it back amongst the others.

Remember to deliver the goods.

Jubilee runs up to me.

With honey they're best—She says, handing me a triangular paper cone with honey dripping down from its tip—Hurry! Hurry! Before it leaks through the bag!—Jubilee grabs three and licks her fingertips.

Ambrosia—I hear Jubilee say swallowing.

Biting into another honeyed date, my saliva collecting(a shard already caught in my teeth)

A fig?—She hands me one from her pocket, pieces of cloth stuck to a sticky wound.
I put it in my shirt pocket.

Declination Road
(on the run)

The garbage in big black bags outside the stalls, cats scurry away and wait, a glass shattering, a dog barking, a lone dark man passes by trailing an unwashed scent.
A metal gate rubs shut, another stall behind its nightcage.
Somewhere a horn bleats lonely at some interloper.

Where are we going?

Down Declension Drive.

Breaking a picked-up leave's spine, my tongue scrambles across its soft green terrain, its bitterness of rock and salt as if I am eating earth. Sephira arrives from an alleyway, picks up the infant's head.

He hasn't filled our eyes.

The nerve patterns—Shuckles repeats.

A fragment of my story without an acceptable way to text.

And he kept searching for me throughout the village, always seemed to be watching, drawn further and further with my ass.

Ah, but then men always watch a woman's ass when they walk—Shuckles says—That and other things—Sephira puts her hand beneath her skirt, touches her ass and laughs.

Mom! I can catch you!

Sephira picks up leaves from the ground, blows against them and takes my hand.

Here, my dear ass watcher and wonderful harassment, eat the leaves.

Filling my mouth with her earth—Chew it, swallow its cement.

From my mouth I cough a spit of her sand.

Be weary of bones—She says.

Just one of your paradigms, one of your schemes—Shuckles says.

I continue roiling the wretched leaves to find a place, my language, my landscape, my people, the construction of events.

To find a scheme.

I lick Sephira's face.

A vague familiarity with the taste of her leaves, the productions that have given birth to my words. I have become a stranger to my meaning. I cannot get it out of my head my mother was only a scheme or a word like 'iceberg'.

At the turnoff down Declension, a green and milkywhite mucus scattered across it

a deterioration(entanglement)I pick my nose and lick the mucus from the tip of my finger, its bitterness and salt(its minerals and pebbles)the dirt that is part of it and the urine that is part of our trace elements. Gagging, forced outward and looking for a drink of water.

Was Sephira my mother?

I look up to the sky seeing the swirling whirlpool of the stars and a quarter moon.

Right, left, lover, mother. It's the same here. I'm still trying to figure out where you are—Jubilee says.

Here?

Here in what I conceive I recoil.

Unable to stop my head from submerging. Sephira, Shuckles and Jubilee breathe an overripe bickering.

I put my finger back in my nose, wet and disintegrating, a little decayed vegetable matter dry upon it. Smelling and inhaling it generously, its scent my digestive juices and the chlorophyll that can change the sun
beckoning me to rejoin it
evaporating in the cooling darkness and cricket thrumming
its sourness still in my mouth
colloidal mumbling.

This—Shuckles holds out two eggs, whole and glimmering beneath the weak dimness of the moon—Take them, they're boiled.
I put them in my bag, concentrating on not breaking them.
In the tomato basket, I see something green, run my fingers over its skin, disfigured with little brown scars. A speckled underbelly with wilted green testicle like leaves hanging at its tip, limbs fused to these wilted testicles(my eyes brought as close as can be drawn)
Laying blind on the earth.
All legs, testicles and arms.
It cracks when I bite it, tasting some soil with the unwashed celery stick.

Take this—Shuckles says putting a spoon in my mouth filled with vinegar, leaves
and sour juices.
Wretching.

Sorry.

Hurry-up! We'll be there soon. Have some crackers—Sephira says.

Why should I take these crackers? This food?
It is your bread
your life
your bread and your life. Soon!

Soon! To the shell. You don't have much time—Sephira interlocks arms, smiling(ruby painted lips and jet black hair)Bobbling.

We have no bread today—She says—They didn't have the time.

Time for what? Who?

Her heavily laced eyes blink missteps, my continuing expansion.

Yes, the time. This market is fleeing. Your hallucination is almost done—She says.

Here is some soup—Shuckles offers a lamb's bone jabbing out beyond the rim, soaked cartilage soft.

Eat it tomorrow. You'll be hungry.

He puts the bone into my bag.

Remember your predecessors—He says.

I try to remember what predecessors he could mean.

Go on Adam. The shell isn't that far and, besides, we're moving downhill to the sea—Shuckles says—We turn off here. Continue with Jubilee. You are getting older and have a long way to cross the waters.

Listening very carefully, I strain to hear water, waves lapping(I hear nothing)my ears stuffed or it is not for me to hear(Yet)But I can turn the corner anyway.

At least.

I see wisps of fog floating like transparent film through the air and smell the salt and dampness, able to recognize its meaning.

It is your bread and your life I remember first, whispering it aloud

It is my bread

my life.

It is our bread and our life—I hear myself say aloud.

Ambrosia passes again somewhere(I smell the sea and her dampness)

Declination

Chasing Shadows

1.

I sit and watch the city

(dried mouth and swollen tongued)

in a clockwise spin

slowly   enlarging

my diameter.

2.

Forgotten how to land, I splash into the sand, froth murmuring amongst the flotsam. The direction of drift jumbled in collusions.

We're going outside the city walls, to the old cemetery.

Jubilee points west, my declension spilling east, beginning our circumvolution.

Why so circuitously?

You've put me into your dilemma and I'm following your rules. Straights just impossible with you.

Kicking the stones as answer.

Worn seahorses carved into the granite of a wall beside a frogspittle stream. Four brown undines jump in, their skin spottled and algae driveling over their breasts, the dim exposure of their eyewhites gestating. Their darkened triangles tempt me.

Little bits of glance become my feeble
mythical vagina
a growing salamander(Efflorescence
caught in my teeth loose and barely cemented(seahorses)
The undines play something vaguely resembling IT, three chase one, climb out from the stream and jump back in, a great flurry of splashings, tongues coiling with laughter, my chest exalting
esperance.

Stop watching them, they're too young for you. Do you want another rape charge?—Jubilee breaks into my meandering—You're trying to get lost.

Look—I say pointing to the undines—Look how they play and laugh so easily.

Playfulness still surprising.

Their cat's eyes flicker, breasts frouncing as they jump

lathering into the frowzy green stream. I try to approach their dark outlines, but they run down a narrow street, the moonlight barely reaching them, becoming even more darkness moving on a darker background(Dreams begin my chase)

Come'on. We have to start dreaming.

Go! Go! Leave me be! I'm dreaming already. I'll follow them and probably'll get to where you're taking me.

Without me, you'll be left here through the night. Perhaps you'll fall into the river. Can you swim?—Jubilee asks.

Kicking the stones as answer.

I puff and huff and fall down.

Picking myself up, I go to the edge of where they had swum. Thirsty to drink.

Frogspittle. It stinks, has no fish. Waterlocked beneath the green, I hear a splashing around my ears, try to jerk my head out, ridding myself of the water as it constricts my throat and begins to drown me, the undines' laughter scattering across the gravel ahead of me. Someone saying from the alleyway—

Please please disseminate me.

Continuations(their darker shades tendentious)

I touch my balls(tight(Man.

Walking along a wall, seven feet high and constructed of irregular stones, pockmarked and weedfilled mortar. I try to remember something of my first scream, something that will help me remember where I am. Their forms play hopscotch, one teetering on her leg to pick up a stone, her meridian a splash of darkness(suddenly feeling one is missing)Not able to recall where she has gone or was she ever here.

We can sit here—Jubilee says.

I have to keep up with the shadows.

Don't be an idiot. Tsit. Shadows always move faster than Man—Eating skin-brown figs and black greek olives—Tsit. Tsit. Don't be an idiot. Shadows are always just ahead of us—Jubilee twangs in deprecation—Why do you mean?

A Place to be Buried

My count reverberates in my bones, straining at the junctures, as if they will not hold
me. Alive as I will die, the pain from up ahead my lifespan. I look for a place to be buried, listening for my evaporation. Pithering after shapes.

Shadows! Shadows!—I yell.

I look for their wings
(as if there are angels
as if there were wings)
I contain the quarter moon and feel the cold stones wedged between two houses.

Jactacious chandelle—Some muttering from a window above. After a few long seconds, I am nearer to them—Jamboree dree—Murmurs from up ahead

Jub.

What? What is it?—I heard my name.

This's further out of your way. Even more roundabout. Why do you mean?

My ligaments ache as if they will snap any step(a tenesmus my atman)
Efflorescence.

Frou Frou.

I am so near falling from the bones
a twittering exhaustion.

A darkness with Sheckanah's breasts and hips comes my way. My head waivering on its atlas, rotating toward its limitations, my back pulling over itself. Folding into myself, I
cannot support its momentum any longer, my skeleton teetering.

Father—I whisper to my surroundings. The shade makes it's way, slides against the wall.

Get up, Stone. You can't stop here.

I do not know where you mean.

Lost in searching for something I can't comprehend(a common destination the incomprehensible)I cannot see(possibly some more of the angles twitting here and forth)Twittering marble centipedes. I can smell their algae frowzy in the breeze. Turning to me, Jubilee's eyes sweep over the gravel path.

The ageless that was Sheckanah is gone.

It was here, coming up the road—I mumble.

Who?

Straining to see any moving blot, but I cannot, only hearing two cats mawling at each other.

If we continue this way, we won't get anywhere.

We won't. Look for a solution to this dilemma.

We won't get to the sea.

My froth

the sea

but I do not remember why I am the only question I can ask. My mind settling on whys(to avoid more limited questions)because I can repeat why

over and over again.

Why can't we just stop here?

You need a place to be buried—Jubilee takes my arm again—An anchorage. You haven't gotten there yet. You've been so sinuous.

Sheckanah and Shuckles appear from up ahead where the undines ran.

Where did they go?

Those were shadows and they died with the sunset.

But I saw them after dark.

You want to catch the din of those four black holes?

Shuckles wiggles his finger level with my wisp.

Why do you keep railing after holes?

I didn't see their cunts—I almost lie—I didn't mean cunts. Holes. Holes.

Because you expect the din, unintelligible and too frequent. Because you do not choose any sounds to follow—I hear from my shell. Shuckles and Sheckanah shift their weight from right to left their skeletons shifting, their rib cage and spine floating
disconnected about their ruins.

What haven't I heard?

Not sure from which skeleton the answer will come.

What sounds you live on.

I hear their collapse, their skeletons' disjoint spread across the gravel, their skulls laying against the opposite wall. I can almost make out their seams.

What can I habitually not hear?

(I only believe I have not heard)

You do not hear the breathing
of the people next to you

(of myself)

sitting
running
beating
as we try to breathe

the heartbeats from

your chest
(my time)
you do not hear the sounds the earth makes
to you
from you
of the insects
on the wind
going by
your skeletons' shoal.
The rains have begun, but I continuously brush the drops away
from my awareness.
What the silence between too much rain means
the sand your body makes
the crack of your knees
the struggling spine
the chorus' pouring.
I sit and rock toward and fro, my spine painful as my head tries to touch my knees.
Why do you act like a priest?—I ask my kith, my voice absorbed by their skulls—For you, this must be a religious event.
I continue dovening, mumbling sounds to see what I can make.
Lalidididimdidimdindurbadorick sundry desiderate but du di du du
din diṇ Fi Fi din
disemboweling
my din—I sing, sounding eventually closer to the rain
badoridundidimdi dddd da dudim pausing for moments with the rain
dudidim ddd dim da dydidy dim di
finding the rhythms of the rain that had begun falling on

the back
of my neck
dim du di dumdi do di ddddddddd didi didi
I follow my ripples continuing past in small splashes.

Canticle

We cannot get to them because they only allude to us, circumvolving round our chase
(myths of ours)
They will go on before and after my living(the closest I can come to comprehend my eternity)I tried to keep these myths at my edges, but they have already infected me(must must they must)There is a nothing called eternity.
The myths and I are entwined.
Drawn nearer, each step brings us closer to our splintering. Pouring to a sewer, our dark liquid slipping toward some disembogue.
I find a doorway near Jubilee and huddle for the storm to pass.

Do you think it will pass soon?

Tasting droplets of rain like wellwater swashing down my culvert. Smelling the earth, my solar plexus hurts.

It can't rain like this for long. Jubilee are you here?

Yes, I'm here. We have to let the rain slow.

My words decline into a mumbling(again trying to correct myself having grown too bobbling)for awhile longer I will remain and recombine.

We are drawn nearer.

I believe we are close(because the alternatives will not sustain me)

This method doesn't seem to end—I mumble.

What method could you mean?

I mean...To begin with...

I immediately know I cannot answer.

If only I knew my text, knew its pauses and footprints, always fading to a point caused but disassociated within.

It(a sunrise's silence shimmering toward my head)

Calm down. Cool down. Take this at your speed.

Idiot!

Idiot!

What speed do you mean?—I talk to myself.

Don't talk to yourself. Don't always try to fill the vacuum—Jubilee says.

Losing my grip, I do not know my speed or method or the direction of my footprints. Exposed awhile beneath the rain fading within the landscape.

What direction have I been going?

Your method and obfuscations.

The black undines slit and swerve in the rain bleary before me.

Who are you talking to?—Jubilee asks, although she should be able to see.

What method will get me started?

Here are our gaps. Grip an ovule and scatter us.

Fill us in

Illusiveness, my obscure palliatives.

Only part of my storm or landscape(my senses and language)could sustain me.

The illusion of possible answers endure around me flagellant in the rain.

Enduring drown upon itself.

Who are you speaking to?

I look into the rain for prayer.

Line text line text line text...—Each drop's sound

emanating from without and within, breaking off in cacophonous noises, reorganizing, again breaking off, the clicking of tongues and foottaps of thunder
betokening.
Already playing out my rhythm.

Please please disseminate me. Grip an ovule and disseminate your rhyme—Their dark bodies ebb in the rainfall.

Line text line text line text...

They continue in answer to a question I can't remember. Biting into a tomato, peering at its seeds, its juice flooding into me. I begin to recognize

Who are you talking to?!

many different combinations of the raindrops, generations of an infinite line of digressions, the pieces of my text. But I cannot go on like this. The undines flower and dissipate in their soundless place, ebbing tide. There must be an end, if only because I can only have so many words(a lie)
The undines fallow with contraries. Consuming the tomato's core, I begin.

You just fell into an infinite regress.

knowingly
(not just I)
Unadmitting.

Finding shelter.

Dissipating into the depleting rain into a wake.

But you don't know its text.

Who the hell are you talking to?!

Canting
offering a prayer
a reclamation a remembrance(canticles)
recapitulation.
I peer at the moth shades and mutter definitions I have

tried.
Meaning only in the doing. Almost as if I am entering the place I was lost within.
Di Di text Dy Dy line Dis

Invoke!

Who the hell are you talking to?!

Jubilee begins to dash toward me.

Can I find my text?

I wobble against the jamb, weak from gnawing, my undertow into a wake.

Be careful of talking to shadows of yourself—Jubilee chides—Passersby will think you're nuts. Besides, we'll never reach the shelter till we move again. Some meaning needs to be agreed to.

I wonder if I can toss my shadows away(myths of mine)If I can redefine some words to get there faster.

Can the shadows become solid?

Only if you make it up. But then they're not always what you wanted.

Wait till sunrise.
Glimmerings only.

Some meanings that assert some place is all you need to continue—My metaphysicians' chorus' pouring.

My foot caught, I tug, but cannot pull loose, jolt my head in the swinge.

The redefinitions are a way for you to function, to continue on in this
world. The myths are the same.

Wrapped in a canvas sheave of words, I sink. I believe I cannot be speaking and drowning at the same time, can hear myself waiting for my shadows to reappear.

You are sucking in the tide—My shadows recall.
(redefining
myths of mine)

Only facsimiles!
I quelch near finished)some sharp recognition
some quizzical recognition.
The undines' shadows in my cant.
Why the hell are you talking, too?!

Gigging Fugues

The rain has stopped. Let's move on.
I must feel that I can understand some grith, or I will create a panic and consume myself. When will I understand?
(already, I try to become giddy from too much breathing)a drug's solicitation.
Let's begin with a few simple, elemental things.
I am a man
(saliferous)I am
Left! Left!—Jubilee slips into a four inch wide cleft between two buildings.
C'mon. It's a short cut. We'll get there faster.
Two testicles
a penis(some dram)
a skeleton
and muscle
The darkness of this cleft so complete I cannot see my hands before my face. A narrow pelvic bone.
C'mon, this's a short cut.
Two testicles
a penis
a scrotal sack
A skeleton
an anabolism
a marrow bone.

a swallow of bile.
A lack of conclusions.
Are they needed for my completion?—I am only—Upon saying this I hesitate

A frame.

Look!—Jubilee sweeps her hand across a vast view as our crevice reopens. In the moonlight, I can only see large darkened blocks providing the illusion of waiting.

An emotional frame.
I go on having no place to sit.
And a brain(with many words)
a semantic confusion.

Where is the penis, the testicles, the seminal fluid?

Hardening as she rushes down

Come-on. Come-on.

the pebbly path.

You should be the man—I say.

Where is your penis, your testicles, your seminal fluid?

The concrete stone I sit upon is ovular.
Impossible to reach definitions in isolation(I must take into account something else, some others)

Who? What? Whowho.

Where is my penis, my testicles, my seminal fluid?
I see some movement on the darkness, a firefly flicking outward looking for a mate(I think of all the sephorim)A light intrudes from a window, barely exhumed I am.

Are you emptying? Are you coming?

I put my face in my hands crouching deeply.

I must give others legitimacy—I hear me say before I remember
thinking it.

But how can I construct my own?

What method will get me started?

Just take what you can't prove and go on without.

There's not enough to believe what I can't prove true.

Is it enough for faith?

A blindfolded man moves to within my sight, my undines run encircling him, jibing and gigging at his side. Circling hectically in his darkness, he tries to grab them, to hook and drag them from his encirclement, gain the energy of one less obstacle to thin the membrane of their enclosing. Chattering with their breath they gig as he tries to grasp them(they grapple at him)some fugues obscured in the darkness.

What are they doing?—I ask Jubilee.

Playing a game with—Shuckles chuckles—me.

He takes his blindfold off.

The children jig.

You must always be prepared to be fooled—Shuckles, the Crown, Mollusk bows, his hair gone at his top.

What happened to your hair?

Being fooled is part of the find.

He approaches, dispersing the children, letting the white blindfold hold taut against his forehead.

I must insure, with a method, that I am fooled only in a precise manner—I mumble, thinking how absurd I sound.

You've always known you were a man but this wasn't good enough. You don't know your function. That's where a bit of your definition lies.

My function(I will set out immediately)

Shuckles replaces his blindfold and recombines his encircling jig of jingling fugues. I search through my head, trying to reclaim my function(but for this I must look outside my cranium)As everything has been.

Will I get there?—I ask.

Go on. You might not.

Grappling for another obscurant, Shuckles smiles at each miss.

No one said you'll recognize the place you're going

Beamlessness

Then you go past.

yackackackackack

1.

I recall walking into some dark density of pines, trying to keep the lights of some shelters flittering through the trees. Eventually a fluttering insect caressed me, the lights went. the sound of crickets and a slowly emerging drip dollop and a voice that spoke to me.
Was me.
Unable to remain quiet, I speak to myself(it must have been for hours, for days)

What will I ascertain by growing past it?—I ask Shuckles.
Yackackackackack—Some bird's song loosed.
Shuckles(my black undines dispersed)Jubilee and I descend the path, rocks crunching beneath our foottaps and ricocheting.
Cricket balm. The intermittent drizzle continues slapping the leaves lightly, pithering absorbed by the ground.
In the distance a car crunches
soil
erosions.

You've always looked for a definition, an essential point or, failing that, some portent. Is there anything so fundamental?
Defining has absorbed my soul(how else could I continue?)First think of some assertion, then a series of steps(trace a line)toward some hopefully lingering point.

Is that all you`ve learned to do after everything? Everything?

What more can I do?

Jubilee explains to Shuckles where we've been, how long it has taken. We have places to go. I keep our progress slow and build

entanglement.

A breeze stirs the leaves as the drizzle stops. I flick some drops from my jacket and search unsuccessfully for the moon through the clouds to see if they are clearing. A shuffling to my right reminds me there are rats. I stroke Jubilee's wet hair and ask

Aren't you cold?

Do you want me to be?

I think what would it matter if I did. Lost sense of function, losing my sense of relevance, the little beats of the drizzle begin again.

Daduda didudi didadu rimduda du fuir dice bet dim rim

La la la la la la...I sing to the clouds, asking them for a song as my berth

and they

la la la la

and they couldn't

la la la

and they couldn't care less.

Are a part of my din.

Jubilee shakes in the damp coolness.

You want me to wiggle?—She asks.

In my while I'll find a route

reflect on a method which insures I can only be fooled one way

reflect on the way.

The accretion of my internal burning(I will have to settle for this)

Jubilee runs into the pervious darkness. Her steps cant a retracing, reconstructing some symbiotic paradigm

with me but not of me(to become warm)
Continuing
although
Continuing eventhough
although
Continuing eventhought
I haven't
Continuing because we haven't any other capacity
but to continue.
The prayers beginning with the relent of wailing, accepted as always having been. My species again.

Rush! Rush!

I hear something above me?
Yes something above me!
(anxiously I study the clouds)
Shuckles smiles the chorus' wailing
a promulgation.

2.

I trip into the darkening soil, my teeth against the earth.

Adam, are you OK? Can you get up—Shuckles stands above me. He holds my bag, slapping off some dirt then wiping his palm flat against his white pants.

Don't get dirty.

It's only your stain.

Rising onto wobbly legs, I think 'move' and they do not move.

Stains have to do with what's left behind, regardless how impermanently you remain on the landscape.

I think that I should go forward and feel for muscular contractions.

A spot in what landscape?

Shuckles gently prods me and I begin to move.

We enter a road surrounded by palm fronds, short and near the ground, their broad leaves darker outlines against space. I look up for the stars, but only see the clouds(I do not even see them but this is the explanation I've been taught)

I assume the clouds
assuming limitations
My hair sticks fastened against my head.
Roots, some latent definition.

3.

Shuckles takes a peanut and cracks its scatterings across his feet, the hulls colored sand into a disappearance.
yackackackackack—Some bird lets loose an alarm.
He reaches the borderline of another space, my judgment flickers dim then out, forcing me to contemplate an edge, Shuckles beyond the next horizon. Only his scattered shells glint.
I chase hulls into a disappearance.
Flickering, the lightning bugs continue to look for mates. Guiding.
A web brushes my face and I grapple with its hold. Counting what hulls I can sea in the direction of the beach, I scrape a palm frond, its sharp edge against my leg. the waves an echo so dispersed, a mere trick of an echo. Jubilee skips a sinuous line, unarticulated. The quiet of her plethora away from my sight.
The rain has stopped and I shiver as the temperature begins to drop, tightening my grip on my bag.

One Two Three Stop!

From the sky, a star is allowed to reach me through time. I scrape my shoe against the gravelly path to sound against Jubilee's continuing rhythmical curvatures.

One To Three Stop!

She finishes another figure eight and spirals off giggling. I follow her spiral into denser space, but there appear only new boundaries delineated by palm fronds and the Chuckchuckchuckchuck on my intine.
yackackackack—The birds stop in a place unrhythmical.

What are you chasing?—Sheckanah taps my shoulder.

Just continuing. Looking for an end. A saving.

I wonder if all my responses to my experiences have been

questions. I wonder if there has been any sort of dialogue.

I am your dialogue—I hear Sheckanah's mirage—What are you?

Sheckanah lumbers with me, my steps slowing to accommodate her increasing size, her inflation having reached a point I could not have imagined, the sheet she wears undulating with each movement, each step pinquinesque.

Are you OK? Why have you continuously grown so?

Why have you made me so?

4.

Each walks round me congruent, Shuckles clockwise and Sheckanah counterclockwise, shuddering. On the air the scent of burning wood. I listen to the waves reclining, retreating, ultimately returning, a light fog obscuring boundaries.

Vultures, the air full of their wings' mumbling. How to understand these circlings.

Their arms clasp and they dance, Shuckles singing in a Waltz's tempo

Ackack ackack ackack Ahrrr Ahrrr Ahrr Ahrr AckAckAck Ack Ackackack dada dum du dem.

Your questions coaxed us and your hesitations allowed us. We will fly when we cannot. Fool you as long as you want.

I will have to discover the way in a discourse, in my actions, or in a desperation, logically to get rid of them. Then what will I have?

A way out.

The Tombstones

1.

Which way to the shack, so I can be rid of us? I am not to blame—I speak to myself in a separate high-pitched voice. Feeling vulnerable with each aspiration, I feel baleful—I haven't control over what we do.
The air seems to waiver between staying aloft or dropping upon me.

Vultures!

We aren't waiting for you to die.
Sheckanah spits onto my groin and I wait for it to burn and
digest me
(but not this spit)
Sheckanah, Jubilee and Shuckles concentrically spin equidistant circles round me
as I follow.

Aren't we going to the shack?

You are the only thing here and we are waiting for our decomposition.
The road has stopped descending. In the distance I can see a flickering light from a small fire and hear the waves of the sear.

That is the cemetery—Sheckanah says.

The shack—repeats Jubilee.

There's a roof over there. Ambrosia's parents are scouring the neighborhood looking for you.
I haven't control over this. Over me. Over this hold.
Over these characters. I haven't control over me.
I can not, not even recognize these characters. Dropping my chest into my ribs, I press into my intestines, con-

stricting the amount of air I can breathe, a mock suffocation.

Do you recognize such depth?—Shuckles says—It is another unrecognized mirage of yours. You should start eliminating these mirages. Become aware of your mirages. You've wanted every mirage you can have.
(to be fooled)

I`ve wanted every mirage that has come to me. Stepping on a paved road, seeing the white glistening lines
(struggling to be seen)

This is the road to the cemetery we were following before you turned into the alleyways(the construction of your text)
A Hyena sniffs my bones, picking at them and acerbic over their ownership.
Wondering what will be my history.
Cracking them for my marrow.

No.

No, not even of myself. Another hyena approaches and they snarl for my bones.
Closing my eyes, I reorganize my breath, hoarse and in deep sallows, out of my control, dry and moistureless. Passing a sandstone with a peculiar round hole through its center large enough for a head.

Put your head in it—Shuckles says—Come, where is your curiosity?
Moving his finger around its lip—I will help you get out again.
I lick my lips with my drying tongue, but it hurts from cold sores developing across its surface in a crocked line
spreading
spreading noward
spreading noward in

spreading noward inward a
spreading noward inward augmentation
spreading noward inward augmentation awareness crooked line
spreading noward
Spreading onward in a crooked line I am.
I cross my chest as if in prayer, turn right, head toward the fire now out of view.
Closing my jaw tight against my sores, I hear the pressure of the stone like the sea underneath, watch the largest glimmerings, reach them wheyfaced, mostly dissipated. Grabbing my head, my eyes roll toward their extremes in my sockets.

I have a headache.

Sweating and my tongue pushing against the right side of my closed jaw I jiggle.

How much further?

Twenty minutes if you don't walk in detours.

Anybody in the shell?

The caretaker lives there. Well, a man who takes care of the cemetery.

I walk only because it is what I have always done not because I am going anywhere.

What about the sea?

It's below.

I find a vegetable juice in my bag and begin to sip it as I walk, disturbing my sores.

Don't drink so fast. You might drown.

I think of being the fog and drifting off and thinning.

One way to begin is with your breath—Shuckles says—And the structure of your bones. Without this, you would've died.

But I don't understand yet and am afraid of misunderstanding. I respire dreaming of recreating.

2.

yackackackackack—some bird lets loose an alarm.
I have been waiting for someone to come, from borderline to borderline, although I did not know it. Part of my situation, convincing myself someone would come. So first Sheckanah then Shuckles came.
I hear the sound of a conch from inside my fist echoing. I will keep what I heave to myself, the sound of splashing surf closeby another conchsound coming from a place I cannot divine. Will I be able to recognize it in the dark?

What don't you understand?

The sear. I want only to look at it.

No change in their encirclement.

Only if the moon comes out very soon.

Shuckles and Jubilee look toward the sky and breath very deeply, the wind picking up the scent of rotting bark. Chckchckchckchckchck—goes the night as I stoop so that my shoulders can press against the wind.

You're always creating hazards, something in your head—Shuckles says.

How did you know what I thought?

Because you both thought and said it.

But I can't remember having said it.

What did I say?

I wonder what's out there—Jubilee laughs.

I am locked in. My eyes blink, avoiding the tearing. Casting peanut shells to the ground, Jubilee and Shuckles offer me some.

They will help you arrive.

Arrive? Arrive to meet what?

Don't you get it? Hansel and Gretel you ass!

Her green eyes startling me.

But these aren't breadcrumbs and the wind will blow them away. Making it unlikely you'll meet those you've lost—Shuckles says.

They both fall beyond my horizon(so I rush to where I think they were and aren't)my borders changing in the windswept darkness so I cannot be sure where they were or I am, only allowing myself to be sure they were close. Thrust forward, I walk down the road, following the reflective lives, street lights skittering. I don't think about possible scars on the roadway, following the broken shells.

but I cannot run

I can barely say

(I am afraid to stop before I am finished)

Wringing my hands till my wrists hurt, I look for their heels. I can't remember how long, the light blurring the few stars illuminating some jackrabbits rushing across the road, the bare outlines of a wind scoured bush.

Why don't you wait?—Angry that I must try and hurry. I collect some saliva and decide what direction is safe to spit.

Don't dilly dally.

In the now thin fog I imagine ghosts pantomime.

Wide open black mouths.

ChckChckChck Ackackackack Chk—Go the birds in the ghosts in the night.

Where are the peanut shells going?

I step on a shell, hear it crack, their heels have disappeared. Only sibilant sounds from the two and the dissipation of the ghosts.

Once I understand what I couldn't hear.

The air no longer so solid, but translucent obscuring.

I thought I saw ghosts.

Don't they hear me? They wouldn't know, for a long time,

if I stopped.
But to where?
Yes, Where?

I must finish—I finally say, feeling some pentup air escaping, relief—

I must finish. I can't keep moving.
To find out where the peanut shells are going.
A note attached to a thorny gooseberry bush reads

Short cut. Short cut. This is a short cut.
I pick up the shells and dream of a cheap trick, intermolecular transportation.
Oneshelltwoshellthreeshellfourshellfiveshellsixshellsevenshelleightshellnineshell

I don't like to be fooled with. I don't want to be fooled with—I murmur(unheard)

Be careful, or we might leave you here and find our own place
to sleep.

Where are you!—Into the now deep night.
tenshellelevenshelltwelveshellthirteenshellfourteenshell-fifteenshell

I would tear your hearts out!
Rustlings.

Be careful or you'll fall over the edge.
Into the past and the future and things of the mind.

Into the rocks—His voice wafts to me with the wind.
I close my fists tightly around my bag and the tomato basket.

I would tear your fuckin' hearts out!—I yell against the wind—Nothing still saving me.
Tightly, too tightly I've closed my fists
and now open them. The impression of my palms.

Be careful what you say—He says—Or I won't

speak.
Absurd I think
absurd.
His voice could be blowing from anywhere and I pick up peanut shells.

I would disembowel you!—My thoughts race, are in thin air.

From the thin air, you will find the tombstones.

3.

Sixteenshellseventeenshelleighteenshellnineteenshelltwe ntyshelltwentyoneshell
Like a fossil, partially buried, two cicadae reverberate in the darkness. I search the sky, the lightning bugs to guide me, but then realize they don't fly so high as I look.
In the wind a tangle of hairy brown weed slaps me(I sniff the wind and can smell its demure)I search my bag but cannot find a flashlight.
I wipe away some shitsmear
twenty three hard to find.
Wandering behind them, trying to find the scattering, trying to stop my
contiguous monologue(small beautiful steps)but incapable. I go forward, each step carefully placed so I don't go over the edge.

How far am I? The peanut shells are gone. I am circling and will collapse and be buried by this sand.

Demureness. You are a creature who carries his own dimunition—Kadman says—But before you go, remember the flames.

Oh, yes. My flames.

Looking about me, I see the flames of the fire again and turn toward them.

I will create a mirage.

Responding by
Responding by my
Responding by my hole.

You mean, you will accept mirages? You will accept the irrational?—He says.

Only if I can't escape with my scepticism.

Cleaving.

Be careful of your way—Shuckles says.

I shiver and crouch further into myself, my shoulders hurting and my hands cold, the tomatoes bumping against my knees. Some dark solids scratch my path ahead and I squint to try to recognize them but the sand hits my face and I have to bend my head downwards and keep my eyes slits. Wandering toward the flickers of light I am willing to pray.

From now I will not touch younger girls. I will believe in you and your answers if you get me out of this. God—I pray insincerely.

Two days!

Two days what?

I remember a time full of myself two days past. A place where the only time was made up of my own inconsistent attempts to keep time. An inconsistent unpredictable time.

Will remembering it make this more explainable?

At least I'll be able to count it.

You already can count on its unpredictability.

I reach the scratches and they are the bars of a gate(where is the entrance?)I have to decide to go right or left.

4.

Bastards!

I grab some bars and try unsuccessfully to break them loose.

Bastards!

I decide to move rightward because I am right handed and I cannot see into the night. How much of what I have done has been done for this reason?

Brushing my hand through my hair, I wonder if I am growing bald, feeling its intangibility and growing stiffness. I look for a brush in my bag and pull hard at the tangles until they break, relishing the pain. I bite into a tomato and watch the flicker from ahead.

Adam! Adam!—Shuckles calls my name, the wind scattering its direction. Its juice runs through my fingers.

How can you be sure you will die, if you cannot be sure I am distinct or indistinct?—Kadman asks.

You are irrelevant to my death—I answer under my breath(surprising myself)

Or your God?

God? Any such thing is irrelevant to my death.

I try to demise if I am right, grapple the black bars passing(having not kept count
unable to concentrate on counting)I look for the moon and see it for a moment before the roof again
closes over me
a tomb
my nights
I must find.
'FIND' turning in my head in three dimensional blocks. The words gone around so long we've forgotten what to find.

Find what?
I inch around a dark pool of water, barely reflecting in the transient moonlight, the earth around it soft and almost sliding under my weight. Droopy, my half eaten tomato in the water, splitting. In the distance, I see something squat, rectangular and solid.
A reality.
How?
A rational necessity(some shavings of rationality)An ending.
(now whisper)
What end?
A fire, a rapture of belief.
(some hope)
I cannot stop hearing the phrase, turning it around.
Some hope—I recognize it is the closest I have to faith.
Find what I've whispered(a part of my history)
find what was said again(as if the mere repetition will produce an answer)
Afraid to take any offered answers as I may be led astray(there are no answers, only questions)
Find what persists.
Finding the entrance gate, a crucified concrete Christ, his cross still dripping from the rain, precariously hanging above each head that has past, will pass. I watch him unblinkingly to be sure he does not fall on my head.
Not this one.
Finding I do not need him. He can be laid in peace finally after dying at our hands.
You're on the lam. You're in hiding.
I always glance at answers, but I do not trust myself, only the trip, the discovering(I think but have not done)
I must have a ritual

a method
a doing.

To what end?—Kadman whispers and I know he is right.

I have tried to deny my own species. It is the way I was trained.

I pass over some grass and come upon tombstones, stopping under a thin birch, its leaves dripping onto me. The tombstone's in the crotch of a pitchforked road, looking like it will lead to the fire. I Hear it cackle. I can feel the sand caught and scraping underneath my twisting steps. In the beginning, we owned the myths(now just pursuing
these)surrounding death.

I feel watched with an immediacy that may or may not be correct. Something I own, the immediacy of our life the rituals of our death(the dances)
I feel watched.

The road moves upward toward the hilltop. In the cemetery pool, manitols, their thickness and girth floating or rolling, break a carpet of plants. Flecks of gold carp that somehow know someone is near begin to clamor at an open corner of the pond
hoping for food.
Only finding shackles of information.

You're going de ripe way. Up—Someone I've never heard before says—When you get to de shmall masholeum wit stone crowsh flying about a cruchified Christ, turn right. All de way to de whole, horahhsh, top.

What person? Who are you?

Heraclitus Hex. You're a'most tere.

I come to the mausoleum, a coffin's length, overgrown, barely six and a half feet high, Jesus' concrete effigy again hovering, pecked at by sculpted crows:

'Forever the Regina Angeloum
Dwells upon this hollowed ground
of these buried Dominions
Wings capped
Poor Poor human remains
Mother of God
Mother of God.
IHVH'—The epitaph reads.

Heraclitus, Who's buried here?—He doesn't hear me against the wind—Who's buried here?

Shame Dominations. De firsht myt'.
My teeth grind and I stop.

De fire isht warm—A gust of wind blows against the graveyard, shaking the surrounding bushes and stunted trees, reminding me of the cold.
'If Only Blessed Be All Who Enter!', reads the threshold.
Stepping upon it, I wonder if I can grope and find the words
anyway
Any way?
Any.
Away(I recall some things will not be in words)those things I search for will not be of words, not even in exegesis.
Another gust of wind rocks me gently, bringing within the sound of the waves and the bleating that is the fire's occasional cackling. This time(perhaps always)I am afraid.
Silence.
I cannot hear the exequies.
(How would they be for angels?)
What kind of silence would it be?
How would it be filled? The wind picks up and paces.

Heraclitus?

Call me Hex.

Yes, OK, Hex. How much farther?

At De top off De hill. Not t'at mush furter.

All my thoughts have been in words(But musn't thoughts be rooted in words?)I sway heavily in one direction and almost trip. I do not hear any answer. Where will I find my song? What will it be? I stop at a grave, habitually reconstructing through my exhaustion its significance. These are the things I must decide.

The Phoenix has gone(for a time)I touch it and consider the possibilities of her death

unpresent

unpresentable.

I kiss my fingers and touch her mound.

Why is there no stone!

What shtone cout you mean? I can barely hear you wit de wint. Bring up...shticks fur...fire.

Beginning the approach, I patter myself for warmth. Without them, I cannot find this trip(must stop retching)Without words I find it hard to be pulled along.

5.

All I know is the enmesh of words—I mumble waiting for Kadman's voice again.
I must find my voice again.
I lean against a tombstone:
Forgery!
Frogery!
His death is a forgery!
If only it weren't so. Sitting on the ground, I turn my head and feel the wind struggle through my stench. If only it weren't so. Leaning against a tombstone, my ashes scatter into obscurity. Having found a comfortable position to freeze overnight, I will not rise, feel the rain begin again.
Hastening me
Du. Di dum.
Di(how could I have known this?)
Dum(UUUUmmm, elongated and present)
Adam! Adam!—Heraclitus shouts barely above the constant rush of the surf against the cliff.
It would be so much easier to jump from the cliff(but then I must get up)
Du didi didi dido deodanddumdum didu didu din dim dint
Looking to my left, the stone reads:
Leviticus:
His innards and his legs
shall be washed in water
to be burnt
of sweet savior.
didiidisembowel
until I've totally exhaled, chewing chichichichi
Devi breathing as I rise.

Geth mothin'! I need more wood fur dis fire!—Hex demands.

I don't recognize the howl, have lost it. Concentrate on the center of my forehead while my eyes try to roll backward, the pounding like the rain on the roof of my catacomb and my back. No matter how I race, I cannot reach him, each step creating no forward motion.

Whach'yer doin'!—Cries Hex.

Trying to reach you, I keep breaking it down and do not arrive.

Gesh on your feet! C`mon, you must get here fur shelter.

Where! Goddamnit, Where!

I remember a time of snow and pines surrounding me, shaken by the wind and wondering if I should move again(shelter was so close)to resist again.

The faster I fractionalize, the further away I will be from this place. Avoiding getting up by this method of thought, each beginning so infinite.

If you don't get up, I'll come and get you—Sephira says.

Within the pines, I mumble something inaudible. I can only hear the wind now and even sometimes the remembered snow

falling into itself.

I hear some reenactment.

Occasionally a fire will start then disappear from the landscape.

Struggling for a fire in my landscape.

Tombstones surround me and I begin to feel our affinity.

In a transverse position I begin to crawl, gripping another tomb, moss splotched and thin, trying to raise myself again.

Breathe in as I grip, breathe out as I let go. This way you won't get too dizzy from lack of oxygen. Or lose

your way in our nave.
Sephira is gone before I can lean against her warmth.
I pull against a tombstone
afraid I will uproot.

Tut tut tut

I find a peanut shell and assume, for the moment, Shuckles and Jubilee are in this with Hex(but then why haven't they spoken with me?)Finding the sacristy, I may discover my penetration.

Arise! Arise! For heaven's sake!

Dead at last.
Dead at last.
Blanching on wobbly legs with the living
leaves batting around me, my eyes wet, my knees almost giving way, a groping staleness in my heart, the drizzle flickering at me. The wind pushes against my movement. Held, I run my fingers over my head, imagine my continuous scar, a bulbous growth, soft and blustery. Sheckanah comes.
Hungrily going from one exigency to the other.
Around a rectangular low stone, I see Sheckanah sit with Shuckles on frail looking chairs playing a board game. Sheckanah an augury, her outlined skeleton poking through the darkness, wrinkled hungry and bareheaded.
Is Hex part of my dilemma?
(only he might not be)
We
We must
We must stop
We must stop lying
We must stop lying to our
ourselves(but
but then what will we have to say? We can have been lying to ourselves all this time
But must speak on. All of it may be a lie(it is only impor-

tant if I do not forsakenly lie)All the lies we make without anything we are sure of.
On the soles of my feet I continue moving toward my mythology. In retching and transitory steps, a methodology for which I can find no better option. If it can be internally consistent, based on some evidence, I will believe(evidence is what others can find, a story others can witness)The rest is faith.
My mythologizing will reinvigorate me.
Shuckles leans forward(as if to respond)Flies and something with a giant long tail snaps and grapples at his flesh. Sheckanah pulls herself up grabbing rectangular tombstones—This is what you would make of us?—She echoes through the swirl created by my awakening—Where are you now?
A bird trembles downward precipitously crashing some twigs in a tree before it grasps a thicker more stable limb. To recoup its strength it throttles in the night

Awhhr Awhhr Awhhr!

I can hear the surf again against the rock and cricket clues, barely able to make a sound blown apart within the wind(I wonder how long I have been away)Can suddenly see the fire flickering in Heraclitus' shelter.
I begin the myths of my world.
di didi didi didu didum uuummm, elongating, finding my voice
in this mimicry of the rain, my lips move ever so slightly and I try so tensely to keep my back from slumping(I begin to observe myself in third person)a momentary reflection.
didi dum dum um di di di di dum dum dum um um um dum dum di diterate dew. Elongated, I bring myself down to some
dreams and the past.

Whorl

1.

Pressing my cheek against a white stone, I feel my nerveending's warmth, coldness returning to my face, my knees shake. I spit onto the grave and soil and splinter on.
The undines with pink ribbons tails flick, their hair skipping.
Flittering buttocks and groins in pink dresses and dark legs past me.
        Come C'mon
One of them sounds like Ambrosia
Thunderstorm clouds
with whitewashed eddies slip
swiftly, racing to avoid the now continuous dolloping of the rain
rancid
toward Hex and the door swinging.
        Skip with us.
        What feels right isn't easy.
        Then perhaps you can't
        keep up with us—The voices pry loose to waiver me on.
Waifish, I hear the sea clench in the finally monotonous night.
From one of these voices and an impinging thigh, I can almost see her
        (I try to prolong her pitch)
        Tut tut tut tut tut
Can do no more than walk to a rise in my cleft. Heraclitus stands at the doorway continuing his tutling

Tut tut tut tut tut
Backlit by some fire(shuffling)
Flinders across his skull and hands
(where are his teeth?)
eyes shimmy a slight shimmering so I know something is there.
Where half you been?
I barf.
Don't you want to
I'm becoming loose.
come out off de rain?
entanglements.
C'mon Comein. We're all here.
I've been crooked a very long time.
Playing catch, Chuckles clutches at the shadow of a head, a roofless edifice of Jesus surrounded by goats along it's path. I try to consider where I will be as I walk in this direction, my chest shirking.
Ship witch us.
A goat mawls overtaking the surf as I breath in my air and stop
(Sup!)
Sheckanah breaches from within.
I touch the walkway concentrating on trolling a dirge.
Some time, I even brought a woman here
of the graveyard
irrigating.
I can finally see his teeth tobacco stained, rent, a plague at the door. I press my nose against it.
He t'at hat an earlet can ear t'at him tap overcomt
I'll hive to t'eat off te bidden Matta or I'll hive 'im a stone and 'is bone, a mew name slitten which no woman know't save she that receive jot.
No meaning retained, no reclaim to go on.

I touch the virulent wall
a reacclamation a
new discovered bend in the curvature of my light(a new name)
I knock at the door.

Half no fear off my meanderthrall. Thish couldn't shtill be shanctified, de lash pilgrim hash gone. Vaporoush by yearsh ago.

Hex makes the sigh of the cross. The diastolic roof sobs, some half twisted torsos naked below my feet in the soil. I have to remember I never believed very hard in my dead. To believe in the peddlings of my dreams'
weepings. Faith is an emotion I must reconstruct.
Had had.
How can it matter?

Why are the goats flying above Christ?

Crosses and spittle.

De anshels are suggeshting...

No, How can I be certain of their meaning?

Only olfacular, ahhh, oracular.

The door between my legs, I look at the angel-winged crouched goats, necks stretched forward and lips back in what might be a snarl.

But these are goats.

They suddenly mewl and one flutters into a tree.

Come. Enter.

Sheckanah's voice breaks against the door.

Lay down your wary head into my mew.

The undines' shadows flitter against Hex's jawbones.

I've forgotten

Forgotten what?

Forgotten how to hear.

Hear what?—Hex laughs, his tooth almost spit—

It wash never imposhible and for now you haven't had

the preparation.
Thinking He is laughing at me, I wave my hand in the semblance of a dying fish
trying to mimic its flapping.

Only a semblance.

Heraclitus swings the door shut.
We are all going.
Closed.
Going where?
Entering.

Enteric remains.

2.

Sometimes I can feel all my pangs shivering
my youth paling
battling against its exhaustion for extension, trying to excite a new formulation.
(Oh, its gonorrhea!)
Whiskering against the askance door boards, I scratch, waiting for the splinter that will be mine.
Mother's finger jiggles through the unplugged hole beckoning.

3.

I wait and search for
a white stone, dig
ging with a stick
befuddling my loam.
Loam of the living.
Loam of the dead.
Rubbed between my fingers it hardens.
Her finger retreated, I am left with the hole.
Inserting my cock.

C'mon, C'min. How long can you diddle?

Drib Drib Drib Drib Drib—Sheckanah taunts—Dribbling Dwaddling Dabbling. I'll put you on my shoulder and you'll spit.
Spitting, I feel the sensation of her saliva moist on my glans.

Dweeb Diddle Dee Dag cock.

Chants pull at my penis violently from the opposite side of the door.
I try to pull out.

Get in here you Dag!

Inside, Sheckanah rocks in the nave before the chancel spitting onto the altar.

Perhaps there was more, but what got through the hole was so little. Search for some addition—Sheckanah blinks—Come and sit here. This's where you'll sleep.

Her head jabs in the direction she spit. I stand in the narthex and find no insects, her scent of marigolds. Through the torn roof I see stars but none shoot.

One head once inhaled is no better than the rest. Your best bet is to stop looking down holes.

But where should I look?

She belches.

Reconnoiter.

I open my eyes wide, try to find some way around her solidity. Undines, Shuckles and Hex hover round the fire. Jubilee takes my hand.

Have a seat by the fire. You need to warm up.

The weight of my baggage drags. A moonlit cloud dissipates past, but I can't find the moon beyond it. I look at my remaining tomatoes and the black fire blink.

Where is the moon? Will this be safe?

Your dialogue is a convenience.

On the altar, opposite the fire, Hex and the undines disappear into reflections.

I look at the torn roof.

What happens if it rains?

We run into the confessionals.

Jubilee skips and jumps in the temporary light of the flame. She laughs. I realize all the stars have gone and wonder at the dizziness of my watching.

Spin with us. Check out our reflections.

Hex and the undines whirl together around the blithering embers as I hear Shuckles' invitation.

4.

They are contemplating my autopsy.
Hazy behind the heat of the fire, Sheckanah sits beside an altar covered by sand, picks with a stick of bone. I sniff long and deep, sneeze. She has finished the mandala of my head. A moth cackles dry in the fire, whose origin I do not understand. I sniff long, but am unable to find the scent of myself. I pick up dirt and toss it at the fire shining too brightly for my resistance, trying to douse the flame and creep closer, my face singeing. I throw more and more slough(old skin tossed)from my eyes(the metamorphosis that composed it consuming my replication)the red ants that were my blood burn orange and white then vaporous. I touch my face.

Get away! You'll get burnt! Are you crazy?

I'm only trying to save myself.

Exfoliation in the wind, purplish and thick, my smoke rises.

5.

It must burn, but it's the smell that gets ya'. It'll rename.

It singed my hair and now I'm...or...

Just smoke.

I can't recognize myself in this darkness. Isn't there some light?

What? In a condemned building?

I need to look at my face.

Forget it.

There's a mirror in the corner there. Maybe it reflects moonlight.

A mirror in moonlight is the form my fugue takes.

Sheckanah pinches my ass—Sit down! Sit down!

I touch my fuzz, wipe across my face my palm, find a pimple, press till it bursts; my reappropriation in the broken mirror. I look into a confessional and believe in the reticence of my skin and bone(the bones of all the dead under this place)I touch it and leave a fingerprint.

Such-a-thing Such-a-thing Such...A patterning. This vision of ruts that makes you distinct.

I will have a look at my face in the morning when I can see...I`ve heard something—I say—Moving toward the fire.

What?—Shuckles asks.

Isn't Phoenix here?

I don't hear her, not remember if I heard her. Hex stabs at the fire.

Such-a-thing, such-a-babushka.

Exhausted, I roll onto my back.

Such-a-bahbahbah

Too indistinct, I close my eyes and try to find her.

A phoenix could be rising from these flames, but it's terribly unlikely.

Douzing(I am incapable of stopping now)

A face begins my sleep.

Fishing

1.

I wriggle about the ocean crosscurrents without a warm grasp to swim in, need to renavigate the subsuming undertows. Dog paddling, pulled inward by my splishings, palings of an artificial compromise, an enforced pantomime. The wind swept particles of sea slowly decompose down my throat.
I am hail driveling and thick.
I look for hope from the drivel, but only imagine replications of old formations
(slowing ephemera)
Hoping my artificial flight will lure me to the lie.
Keep me from being pulled past.
Keep my sand from blowing inarticulately.
Sump sump sump go my heals. My mandala at the horizon, emissive.
Trying to find the sum of my walking, reading my footsteps like tea leaves, but they are translucent, distorted by cracks in the stone they sit on. I move to the next eradicable bandaging, always onto the next crumpling each time I step.
My jellyfish eyes follow my flyspeck.
Heraclitus spins round the earth(my eyeballs liquefy dispersing in my forehead)
saplings begin hitting the surface.
I wait for the rain to become mud and adhere
to form a splint of land.
My forehead begins to pound as the pressure bears on my grot brains.

You rapped—Says a vague stranger with a gold

tooth in a worn gray aquashimmering sports jacket.

Raped? Raped who?

Rap Rap, ape. Ape. Sap!—She slaps me. I try to remember who she was but can't—Rapt your gist? Are you fishing?

I've never fished.

You`ve got to stand straight because your back will hurt if you don't and you've got to jerk the line and wait till you feel the vibration of a bite tugging. Everyone has their own preoccupations. One of them will bite.
Fishhooks descend.

I will wait for you because I must be caught by you. I have no choice. I will wait for you.
Organizing my back, searching for some libation in the line.
Catching a starfish, I chop it into five fingers. Each will grow into another. A whiskery fish says—Look at you floating there bobbing to and fro like a Jove departing.
I am a fisherman.

2.

My line tautens.
I wipe some of my salt, penitent crystals failing
unbidden
erosion of images in an attempt to create an other.
Absorbed in the sea, I feel as if I'll urinate in my pants, lock my penis between my legs to wait. A salt pillar looms ahead full of crustaceans that can only tolerate a lack of current. I try to smell and taste the night I have called my nothing(there isn't any recognition)My sperm.

You've forgotten your bone. Let the fumes escape, the garfish take the line. Feel the soft coolness of the ocean as you begin to swim. Submerged, reemerging. Your line trying to discover the process. Not capturing a fish, you follow it bobbing to and fro above the coral reef wondering where all the fish have gone.
None bite the lure.
No affirmation.

Here was the escape you were searching for; you must repeat the bobbing until an affirmation
bobs and tugs.
I begin my rhyme in the swells. A mudfish moves in the scattering quartz, no cause for its locomotion.
Puffing up and ready to defend, a porcupine fish moves toward me, recognizing my fate.
I wait the line
in a fug
nibbles come and nibbles go
a gar does not take hold, but some weed
The hook searching just above the darkness.
The porcupine fish addles toward me.

3.

I shuffle through the drab bled liquid, my change running out in dribs and drabs. In the dark, a clownfish provokes the poisonous fingers of its anemone, having found me. I scan the surface, the river's suffocation our last tryst(we kissed)an orgasm blew my nook. I feel the weariness beginning Phoenix's siphoning.

Why do you row me into this morass?—Phoenix asked—Fish for something fertile and rich. I won't remain beside you for long. Find the muscle.

I'll go fishing. I'll catch something and bring it home.

All you bring home to eat is skives. This's where they'll bury us. Pauper's ground. Funeral poor—Pointing to an unyielding ground—There may be an end any time.

I pick up the alter sand and let it run through my fingers a poor man's death. My boat struck a drowned collie, entangled in my line. I dredged the river for the master with the body of his dog, tongue swollen.

Lapping
until eventually
until eventually I
until eventually I may
(may or may not)
until I eventually will
understand, be the master.
Staring into the precipice I have created.

What precipice is this?—A sudden Unlocated voice asks in the landscape of my dream.

My nose bleeding, dribbling into a shallow pool, picked apart by the currents. Pieces of myself falling where no words are successful.

No choice as each part hits the pool in which direction I will go.

4.

The starfish's arms inseminate
the garfish's jaw clamps shut
the purple porcupine fish deflates
I breach in shallow water and not well.
Recast the line, watch it plunge into the dragging river
scoriaceous and streamless
(even placidness can be an answer)
An answer in a language one can adhere to(but I
cannot even dance to it.
I pump the line
soundless, avoid looking
over the rim at it'
sssss wordlessness.
Where has everyone gone in the wide expanse of my
mutterings?
Is it even a dream without others?
Whispering again, unexplainable in the landscape.
A new mooring toil fer t'other.

5.

I descend to search for the meaning on the back of an ass without any wind heading toward a barren plane but for a speck of Phoenix and another sunbathing. I roll over and up to the wall and pee.

We have a bathroom, damnyou!

I forget this as I fall back asleep, absorbed by the flatland, dreaming the land breaks over me wet, submerged in the colloidal sand and salt filled sea sweeping into my ears.

The ass haws very loud far beyond its depth.

Rising above the wave, I'm near the beachhead. I run my hands over my skin, feeling the sea's slickness.

Why did you follow us here?

Phoenix boils very loud far too deep.

Toes tingling from kneeling on my haunches.

You've got a blister.

The prone figure on her right is me, a blister on my back.

I touch its liquid shift

daydream of tearing it open. I press and press again, hoping it will break.

What're you doin'?

Looking for an infection.

What name are you now? What name are you now?—Phoenix sings like Happy Birthday.

Don't you know my name?

At least not mine—Phoenix rises and waddles a step that threatens failing

Fragile bone.

I try to catch my nonce

my arms swagger, legs swindling, reach for my new name.

But you know—Far away I hear Phoenix, though within the circumstances of this beach, she is so near.

time is passing.
Phoenix pulls gently at my arm.
And you'll only have the energy once.
My blister bursts and I retract, twisting and pressing into the sand, too late an attempt to escape or absorb my cloudy liquid.
Get a 9 to 5.
A 6 by 2?
My white stone falls off the precipice
& is unseen.
I said A...

6.

The pieces of my identity construed, entropic, sitting on an islet, watching
the cusp of the moon
my time taking shape
and still I hardly breathe.
Forgotten how to land, I fall off my ass, a frenzy of mosquitoes rush over me, examining to see if their mirage is alive
Leech.
Attempting to smell a moth's zigzagged flight to my innards, forming a cocoon whose outcome I cannot even speculate, the glint of brightness from the world something intrusive. Rolling like a dune in the slow winddroning, decapitated and rebuilding daily landscapes, crescent burns from coarse dust, unable to escape my heredity. These formulations found in the birth(two worms locked together in the clamp of their secretions)a thick fertile perspiration skeletons and eggs dormant, mingling in the waves of my ground.

Wattle! Wattle! Where is the watt...I mean water, I'm sorry.

There's a drinking fountain at the edge of the precipice.

I still need to witness. Up a steep mud and stone trail on the side of the cliff going back to the precipice I had somehow left, yellow and purple honeysuckle and Leander and the donkey's last haw.
I watch her buttock's momentum, my mouth tingling dry.

We have to get there.

The precipice?

The burial.

Bugs emerge with the ascending moon.

We surround the pit, the dead body's victuals in a jar beside its right, Sheckanah to my left, Shuckles clicking his tongue(he cannot stop now)A burlap covered chill that tells me Phoenix is below me. I do not look at the precipice(Behind me)
the moon dispersed, a deep black drop.

I thought they didn't use this graveyard anymore?

They aren't.

Rising from my sleep, I hear Kadman from below wispering phantoms behind my head. In many voices he fabricates a continuation, fabricates a story.

Stone, why didn't you just follow the straight and narrow? Your points are dispersing.

I fall back asleep, hear Kadman's voice and listen.

THE CLEAVAGE OF GHOSTS

1.

Stone is unsure of the spent earth(a dead grasshopper in his path)Before his barefeet can reach and traverse his bald state, ignorant of what he carries.
Spiraling close, I tell him—Don't move don't expect.

Why did he come? Sleeping where I usually sleep, his jowls jumbling dreams, something incendiary. A cat's muttering as if his skull lay next to mine and I can't get away. Shut him up! Stop masturbating! Ack! Always chewing. I want to wake him up. He was alright in the head till he began looking for a little meaning, meandering grasp through rain, reaching this jaundice. I used to know him but am now just a part. He's fallen apart. Started on solid ground, right foot two feet, march. But then he lost it, tripped. And I helped trip him. Once he disassociated me. After all, I wasn't supposed to be disassociated, a problematic entity. I was copulate and congenital once, considered a real beauty, when unremarked. It's those remarks. Once he made them, the doubt can't, I mean, be taken back. When we were young, we were unconscious, cloudiness, cumulus nimble or something like that. Now, it's like trying to find a phallus that understands—Sheckanah begins.

Why not sleep with him?—Shuckles points at Stone sleeping.

His cranium lay next to me, his mother's femur. Stopped trying to cast him out, released my cleavage. From the beginning, our skin dragging against the bone—Sephira shakes her head at him.
Roils from the distance splashing in a concussion. Silt waits for the undertow against the onset of tide. An overgrown mole burrowing tunnels that cave away as he passes.

T'won't get'im. Begginnin' in de mornin', you won't be shpoil'en to wake'im more. Heal sleep till the tide reals'im into shome net. Ya won't have'him no more to critik. He'd been a troublesome boy. Why'nt face it—Hex blows his nose at the fire, but misses—I knew'im ten—Hex touches Stone with his index finger.

Stone fabricates cleavages that hang many generations. Distorts his forebears.

—I knew'im ten. Wash wretched ten. Couldn't shtan' shtill for anytin', always wanderin' the shtreets lookin' for shomethin' new, the stain of the reinactment off a cause, the cause always nearly the shame, identical, not even dee happenin'. What was enough about it wash carried ignorance. I haf'ta recognize am ignorant hoot.
Sheckanah flaps her head, an undulation runs through Stone's foot.

He shited on me knee an astht if I knew a way he could get to the monoliths. I knew a'way dat gut ath any.

Get those damned teeth fixed!

Stone always tried to see the faces and grab at the ghosts cantankering, cleaving to his ghosts as if they were the necessity of living, the only necessity he believed in. Come close to the surf that he might breach some beach. I remember my screams at his teething. I tried to cast him out when began chewing on my breasts. Bit down so hard, chewing like generations before. His hands always extended and trying to grab my nipples—Sephira throws a twig into the fire, flaring.

Breached your tiths?

He constructed himself so meticulously, till he had created a game without an endgame, relentlessly. It burned down. All he does is isolate his parts! Dry his thing. He had to prepare himself, but he kept dissipating. Seamen skills. From that park urinal he came bobbing out, a cheap magician pulling a fast trick. If he had any sanity, he'd've recognized us. This whole damn game's afraid of us, each and every move lets his wants dissipate. What with all the time and place he could fuck up. Only those with elegies make it—Sheckanah shuffles the cards, resituates her buttocks on the granite—Look at his hands always arresting his cock!

Not my son! It's only natural his hands rest there. We used to sit on our hunches, all of us with our hands resting there. There ain't no problem with that. He's just resting, my child rocked in my lamp.

Febrile bitch!—Sheckanah yells at Sephira.

Weeding to find his ghosts. Whimsical. He holds on to his homunculus. Can't let that man draw in the drink. It must be that time he fell off the swing at full sprig, wasn't even holding on. Lost his breath—Shuckles joins in.

I whisper in Stone's solar plexus—You shouldn't have even begun.

Jubilee watches the fire, coal mostly white, blowing it red. Stone
Tried to hold
tried to breathe
and to call
& to speak
to his dreams winding about him(I grope his pate)In the

body we share, our fingers crawl to the edge of our thinning hair. He hears the oncoming sounds of traffic, rubber pulling toward him, rubs his empty palm through me, to get rid of me.

The information's traveling fast. He's gonna have to move out tomorrow—Jubilee says to the general assembly.

Stone grazes over a broken string of pain dangling in the middle of the highway.

Shuckles looks into the fire.

What'd you say Sheckanah?

To remember. That's why I won't sleep with him. He wakes up and doesn't even care to remember a dream. He knows that some of us will be awake then, so he doesn't. Some of us might appear when he sleeps. That's another reason he forgets, can't face up to anything. He always has, since I've known him, been looking at points to reach, then spitting wide around the answer. He's so full of blabber.

Essau chases Ambrosia round the fire—Was it a good fuck?

My son's not full of blather. We can't let him be found. We've got to save him from the cops. Now, he's been confused.

Was it a good fuck?

Fitfully, in the good 'ol days, Shuckles and I'd take him to temple some Saturdays. Tried to pave the orchestration. Now, he'll have to start all over again. It's like he's never been suckled.

Stone pushes threw another breaking wave toward shore.

Ambrosia throws a rock into the fire.

None of your damn business! We can't let him be found. After all, I wanted it too!—Ambrosia screams.

Tree police fish'ere in'he mornin'. They alwish

been comin'up and dey will continue dare pattern. They alwish clash me away. He'll'ave to fitfully continue lookin' till we be found.

My son's not a tree!

Dog dag wee, what was it you were lookin' for again? Ain't recalling? Some feed, couldn't sneeze?—Stone says in his sleep, mutters at his family gathering, unregurgitated. Even replicas share some patternings with the original.

I whisper to him—Because we gave you this—Drowsing deeper into the mire, he remains asleep, his hands splay, the ground between his fingers rushing forward into the living.

Speaking! Speaking! Snoring! I'll never fall asleep! Him sleeping with thirteen year olds bringing the police on us! He aint got no elegancies. He'll do almost anything just to get on. Eventually, he'll make things up. When I first met him, he'd said he'd wanted to say everything with gibberish. God what gibberish!

I whisper to Sheckanah—Mama, Let him sleep! He's had a long day.

No one but Stone hears me.

We 'ave to tinker weed 'is hiding. We'ill find'im if we twy. Tuck'im under de arsh of de comfeshionary box. Ambrosia just before leaving kneels.

My first lover. He looks so calm and so much younger asleep. We're together, he said we would stay together. Why can't Dad understand? I wonder what will happen to him? I have to go home soon or my father will be madder'n heck.

He has to search
to aspire
to revive a head.

Let's play poker.

In the dark?

Throw another log on the fire.

Throwing some pebbles in his mouth, Shuckles feels for his scrawl and the fire flares.

2.

Spitting-up, Stone regurgitates a little bile then swallows.

Great. Five card, Joker's wild. Who will we bet?

Don't you want to get up and play, Stone? Can't you hear us, Stone? It's not only through chance that you reach your destinations. There are patterns even in chance. And you wanted gibberish. Instead you got us—Sheckanah laughs hysterically and in the burst coughs from deep in her belly, tailend of her brawling.

Stone strains to see his route so that he might find a sign with his destinations' name on a highway surrounded by the night images of a dense forest, even though, if he found a sign, he wouldn't be sure it was the destination. Turning over in his sleep, onto his belly, he whispers—Uh?—I hear his heartbeat through the ground laying prone.

Who wants to deal?

Sephira is confused by Sheckanah's stakes.

What are we betting?

Best out'a five. If you win, we continue to hide him. If I win, we feed him to the pigs. If Hex or Shuckles wins, they get to decide.

Why do you hate him so much? He hasn't done anything to you.

He's trying to get at my pudendum and he's dreaming. We've followed him around and waited for him to understand, but he hasn't. He's constantly remarking on this or that, but doesn't know what he's talking about. Then, when he formulates some possibility, he falls apart and says he can't make it so. He'll give me a heart attack! He gives me heartburn.

In the tube of everyone's trachea is all his remaining air,

but the chorus continues to splash about him. Stone's lover played sleeping beauty, young and soft, thirteen years old, puckering up and waiting(clung to his side after the game as if she might lose him)thinking of games beside the tenement buildings. Underneath the El, the older sister threw a kiss to the train her lover left on. The trains slogged past repetitively rattling the ties. He stops hearing the trains and hesitates a moment in his dream wondering why there is no sound. The young girl by his side pulls his sleeve, but he doesn't see her. Stone falls back into the uncovered trolley tracks, a red light glimmering from a fried chicken sign, reflecting in a pool of water from the recent rain.

Don't you adore our moon?

Flush.

A full house. You got that hand, Sephira.

Nothin'. All this searchin' and nothin'. Me and Stone ain't got nothin' to play.

Jus'a pair. That ain't right.

In order to breathe in the light, he is drawn to the dark, surrounded by his view down the precipice, spiraling down toward his head(hunkering)wondering from where he was dropped. Stunted around him lie trees and a rural road, the smell of cow manure. Stone pulls himself from the flat of his back. He must try another route, many sentences remain unfinished because he has not been able to reach them. He turns around, the dune grass blows amongst the tossed unkempt gravestones
but if he moves
but if he moves
where can he go?
Surveying for a landscape.

3.

Are you in? Are you out?—Sheckanah asks.

In.

You can't give in. You've no right. We raised him! Sephira looks at her first card.

He's grown up and got lost, become a nuisance to his kith and kin. Found material is all we are. Can only stumble with us. Get up! You scum.

He's really not clear enough to find us yet.

Can't do anythin' but leth him shtay. We mush go on till he dishcofers our relationship.

Shuckles raps the table. Hex throws his card at the table and everyone sees his ace.

You've lost your ace you fool!

Quiet! Quiet! We can't continue playing if you're at each other's throats—Shuckles says.

Get up! Get up you pile a' dawr. Get out of our house.

What house are you talking about you fool? There ain't even a roof. We're waiting to be sneezed asslide.

Shuckles flicks a piece of dirt from the table and searches for an ant to kill, puts his cupped hand to his mouth, waits to sneeze.

Don't steal, he stole. Don't bother, he bothered. Don't burrow, he burrowed. Got himself into that shit laden pissed-in hole.

Slid sligh slid—Sephira says.

Now look at the mess. Went from stealing to fucking! This crime spree is growing more intense—Sheckanah says.

Sliding into what?—Shuckles asks.

Dissolution. He slid from a whole—Sheckanah

scatters the deck on the stone—That's right, slide into holes!

We got to save him. He's our progeny.

No, he's not. We're his.

Just look at what he's made of us!

Think what it'll be if he doethn't find a routhe.

Hex opens his fly, scratches his penis.

Put that thing back in your pants you filthy scum!

You use shcum fur too offen.

I've had it far to often—Sheckanah tries to continue the game—The same for all these men, keep sliding in and out. Repetitious salivation.

What's the solution? Are you gonna deal or is this hand gonna end?—Shuckles asks.

Solutions, that's right. Solution after solution and look where this lacking has gotten him.

I'm out. Are you gonna deal or is this the end?

Why do you want to turn him in?—Sephira has two kings.

We wasn't built for this. Goddamnit, I don't got but two breasts. Big as they are, I'm not enough to feed him alone—Sheckanah has a pair of queens.

Save yourself. Stave yourself. Your mother's teats are dried oblivion—I mumble, intersect in his dream and there is a confusion of frames.

Hex only has two fours.

An angelgoat comes in through the door and bays.

He slept with a minor. Whose father's lost his head. Can't say I blame him. Then he takes this other man's tomatoes and doesn't even return them. He's been wandering around all day with all these bright red balls and a suitcase. And he just still don't get it. He keeps looking for one of us, particularly me, since I've got imaginable cunt and your cunt, his mother, is just some hot gas.

Unimaginable.

Isn't that what he's doing now, unimagining?

What kind of a conversation is this?

Deal, for Christ's sake! Just deal. We've got to keep the game going.

It won do shear, Shuckles. Got any anshells to spare t'raish de sheaks?

Got any Aces to spare?

Maybe thatsh why he come here, lookin' for anshells. He shure been burning ash of late—Hex says.

There ain't no angels in a deck'a cards.

Joerk'sh wild, so could be.

The angelgoat begins moving around the church, spiraling toward them. Another goat follows through the door and drinks holy water.

Before, he was just ignorant. Now, he's begun scratching and he tots some infection. It all goes back to his toilet training—Sheckanah says.

I did a good job pooping my boy! It—

It wasn't hard poping your boy! Get out! You, you, Incubator!

If I only could incubate. If I only were alive.

The undines run up to Stone with a stone, put it beside his feet.

In the haze through the torn roof the moon bores orange, careening to the next hot day. Stone watches the moon stay ahead of the moving car, swerving and sometimes skimming the trees alongside the road, always returning to a fixed point in his movement, ebbing but not disappearing. Reaching out to touch it, his hand passes through the glass of the window he knows is closed. Stopped for a moment to look at the empty outline of his

arm, he reaches, but cannot keep his sight fixed. Until he retreats back into the car, he cannot bring back the solidity of his arm.
Still dreaming the road he feels a fall.
I ask Stone—Is it dead?
He impugns the sweaty night, wants to get back to where he was spun from, watch the patterns of his communication. All he can see through the trees is the moon, a large orange ball.
I ask—How do you know?
He tries to get in amongst the trees, but the underground is too thick. Feeling in his pockets, he looks for a fruit, its skin smooth but beginning to wrinkle, considers the sounds fleeing from him, the mosquitoes attracted to him.

Your bones. Your bones. Carry them. Take them! Take them!—The Undines sing in his ear. He covers his head, but they pry his hands off.
He digs out the fruit and it is a dull sliver of chicken bone, black and ivory shrieked, exploding in his gums. Swallowing his bleeding, he is reminded of his vulnerability.
They surround and poke him—Alibi! Alibi! Alibi!

Two Pair—Shuckles says.

Only one.

A straight. Hah, another!

Sephira wags her finger at Sheckanah.

Be careful where you point it honey, it might get dirty.
She laughs, coughs and grabs her belly. Stone grasps a tree, but still has no control over his walk. He drops the bone, but it will not dissolve back to the darkness. He leans against a tree and slides onto the ground. Only the children can take the bone back—We give gifts here to

strangers—He hears the chorus sing. Ambrosia smelling of soil comes for him, smiles and says—Can you give me candy?—He digs in his pant, cries that he may not have any rain left. Ambrosia doesn't believe and he tries fingering and she slaps his butt, her hand half his size. After she leaves, he wonders if he could find more for the little girl, coming in a small and mildly painful solution.

Can you give us something more? Something more than your scum. This is your space. We want what you can coerce—He is surprised he can hear the grass in the breeze from the horizon. Before he could only hear the voices but no movement.

Deal!—Shuckles screams.

Impatient man! I have to find all the cards. I dropped them!

Stone tries to salvage himself, the colored sands of his replication slowly blowing in the shifting tide, the string of pain along the highway scribbled in the faltering burial headlights—Where is this car taking me?—Stone asks the back of the driver's head—Rushing through the glaring streets. Chased because you had to cum. The police pursuing you, Prick—Dementia in a clenching of his hands. He feels pin-pricks in his soles—Driver, could you turn around? Driveller hey! My feet are falling asleep!—He leans forward and sees that there is only a vinyl head and torso, to fool any one looking in.

You're it! You're it!—Chasing them round and round the odleayee tree, peeled back bark, unable to catch them.

Unable to catch them.

Ciphering the chorus' scattering(it's roots in sad rolling waves)The sand rippling in between his toes, blather and nettles agog in the wind. Bungling an oncoming spore at

the edge of his wrap, trying to find his ground in this murkiness(colloidal ocean dust)swimming an impossible ballad.
Adam whines in a dream—Stone's in it! He's it!
The blind twins break out of the chorus. Pulled in by the game. He completes another movement of his involvement, tries to catch them, no longer just watch them scattering around the odleayee tree.
Underneath a steamy armpit, a slug after a rain. Fingers incessantly splick splith splick splith(the salt spray of the sea)a scattered corpse.
Sheckanah has sixes—Damn it!—As Sephira revels in her full house.

Jus'a tryst—Hex says.

I never in my life incested my son.

Incest ain't no verb. He can't be put out anyway—Shuckles says.

Why not?—Sheckanah wants to know.

Ol' lady, he'll bring down the tree police.

Oh'me God!

I ask Stone—What'a you gonna do? What?
Sephira has five of a kind.

Impossible! Damn it, I'm losing this.

With a wild cart, anythin's pothible—Hex mumbles—There coot be anshells in the deck.

Another goatangel walks in, flies to the exhausted fire and sniffs from a safe distance. Out of breath, another flits from the Heaven tree growing in the middle of the shell. The goats begin to move in tightening circles round the card game.
Stone's chorus offers a small and thin waiver of sunlight—Eat it! Eat it!

I'll make tith shocker an anshel.

There ain't no angels in cards—Sheckanah persists.

Anshels are more powerful than aces, kings or queens.

You can't make up a new card! It's cheating.

Make me.

Pushed a little closer to Stone's exhumation.
As the rules change, they try to push out the seams, thick and full of themselves. He opens his eyes, then closes them again, all dark and there is no sight but the sounds of cicadae, cricket, and the surf. A mosquito. A covenant too unformed to be immediately grasped waits
intermingles.
Stone picks himself up. Women wrapped in sheets pass him and do not even look at his wrangling or help in this effort to get up from the disposal. He claws hard toward a small affirmation he half recognizes, digs a borrow, spits sand from his mouth and rubs his tongue against his gums to clean loose particles. Imparted from the sand, blown to disentangling.

I've got three kings.

Only three queens.

Nothing but a pair. It's not my night.

You win Hex—Sheckanah says. She tosses her cards without saying what she had.

Like a mole not watching the caving in behind us, trying to ignore the knowledge that we can't go back.

After many generations, we evolved eyes, see walls up ahead. I'm glad we've looked for it—I say to Stone.

He doesn't believe it and tries to dilate his pupils, gain more light, see images in the wrong place. Pointing to the gray evaporating tunnel beneath the rain da da du didi-dida da da da du di dididi du du du du
I say—Di
He will catch his Cipher.

4.

Stone no longer feels the surge of his youth. Still not too late, he looks for hope in his middle age, the chorus dispersing around the trunk of their source.
Not stillborn.

Deal!

I'm doing the best I can with the situation at hand. Five cards have been burned. Besides, you haven't won one damn hand.

You deal like shit, Sheckanah. Luck's not on my side tonight—Shuckles grabs the cards hastily, as if they are an answer.

Neither me. Do you think you're alone? Don't think you're alone Stone, you shit. You never could ask others for help, always buried in our dirt digging crater after crater. Found a clue here and a species there. Believed in the fossil remains scattered, but forgot. Forgot Goddamnit!

Don't use the lord's name in vain.

The lord is in vain.

An angelgoat flies in through the ceiling, a halo round its neck.

That must be an important angel.

I win cause I got two off a kind.

Wait a minute, I've got a straight and a pair.

But one off my pairs ish anshells.

There ain't no angels in a deck'a cards!—Shuckles screams.

Hex throws down his two jacks.

Anshells.

The goats move to the pile of tomatoes and begin gnawing at the basket.

The children babble, pass around Stone, tightening a cir-

cle.
I tell him—Everything is not lost.
Watching the angels swelter amongst the Heaven tree, nothing to do, too many and too vague to catch his reflections in their dance that draws nearer. Grey flotsam twists round his curvature of place. Descending to scratch an itch, he follows his adhesion(pale vein)Admits he knows nothing of the present. A tingling groin caws, flouncing in the scent sliding toward his calves.
Ivy reaches for his eyes. What he can not escape. The buoyancy of his youth tumbled down a ditch, over a main artery, unseen in the dark forest, limbs frantically circumscribed. The flotsam strikes his skeletal frame, shaken. The underlying shadows converge upon him; he awakens, his abdomen so tight, he has trouble breathing. He looks around to understand what and where he is falling, at the characters converging, at the fire just smoke, crickets charade, a cat-bird's prayer. He was scavenging, until he could not help but crash, waiting for a ghost.
The impact of his dream has left a headache. He puts his hand over his forehead and goes back to sleep. Nothing above nor only a bellow. The impact and wet leaves cover his face.
The flotsam, the undines, the fire is gone.
I touch his forehead, the glimpses passed. Lege's large women tumbling in a blank sky. Dismembering. He doesn't watch the cavein amongst us, turns over, reaches a totally dark spot, bereft of all space and thought of time. The hoofed chorus circumambient around the poker game.
He pulls himself from the hole and walks further into the woods, to a steep hill, begins to zigzag, habitually searching for the least resistance.

I say in order to slow him down—You have covered so little space, trying to find the rhythms.
Stone looks around for something familiar, sinks monotonously into the soft ground. He stops, listens in the dark, sees a light, marmalade and dispassionate behind trees and follows it further into the woods. Reading the top of the hill, he looks for a mark, but can pick none.
Jussive undines hide, tantalize—Why should I follow you? What? Follow you to the river? Why should I follow you?
I answer—We guide you and you know not where else to go.
He continues to zigzag in the wandering, grabbing behind trees for the hidden undines, trying to see a piece of earth that might look like a path.

Do I have a choice?

A goat flies past the moon. He looks up, feeling its shadow and hearing a wing flap.
Had not seen.
Had not moved.
Look See?
He sits in a covert
against the rot of a tree. Moves pale and hardly breathing, each step a sideways shift, chewing on grass stems to quench his thirst.

Ha!

What are you laughing at?

More anshells more anshells

Damn these angels. I won't play if her persists with these angels!

Shuckles, are you in or out?

Out!

You're cheating, Hex.

I'ff a right to cheat in my own backyard.

When he was younger, he wrote some things and then hid them. I wonder if he knows where we are?

He's waiting for this dream to come to an end.
Water spots in his eyes, fossils first mistook for answers.
Increasing his contrivance, he craws along exposed roots, unable to see, the scent of his face, the scent of his rumination(a reminder of his burial)
Stone casts a thread to his unknown ancestor but he cannot reel him in
his thread, our scent.
I hold his line.
I say—Reel it in
He hasn't enough
not enough to appease the goats.
Dismembering his expressions till he doesn't bluster, quiet and meaningless. In a worm fit of rage, his shallow root navigates, tries to find a dry spot. A shadow paces, brown in the night, dragging a tale, ears twisting to hear what he will say. Stone can hear the last train rail at some distance, the end of a weal.

NaNaNaNaNa, you can't catch us!
On the assumption the light might lead him to a reliable scene, he stumbles, scraps his knuckles on the bark of a tree, snatches at others. Again, he wakes up, holds his head, goes to the altar to stop this.
Into the next mirage, an ever decreasing diameter surrounds him.
Out of the distance, he hears a river rummaging. He hears his chorus howling like a dog—Step inside.
He closes his eyes before the altar, a slug after a heavy rain, slick and gray and just recently fed. Oil-streaked slowly shifting his weight on his knees to pray(He doesn't understand why he believes things he cannot imagine what they are)

5.

Tumbleweed deeper, rolling through the clarinet's barking. A dog's howl on the verge of breaking behind the night. The moon like a candy apple bitten, Stone's gums bleed.
Falling woman like rain(a deep hazing ferment)
Herded women drenched, their weeds rattling, forming equatorial triangles.
Blisters on their backs(a white drink)their stench.
Blisters on their backs.
His tongue tries to reach their bowels
of manna.
And we are
And we are on
and we are on the verge
on the verge of
the verge of a collapse.
A dog's howl breaks into carrion.
In the darkness, the undines move, hiding more deeply behind the trees.
I say—Sit here.
Bidding his time, Stone takes a seat by a large hole in the wall, evolving into another place along the text. a lingering place.
He thinks, Only here. Only here.
Stronger because he doesn't care if he lives now, only that he moves on. The woods hum round the card players, mosquitoes and lightning ricocheting about him, flies surround his head, behind his eardrums.
I do not speak. We watch only the flies.
Getting up, he watches them rush upward aware of his movement, into the night sky, everything so dense for a blind second, all seconds blind in this sky, as if only the

swarm see. He slaps his right then left cheek, then his forehead. The misquitoes brew away again.
Geometrical and thick limbed, his relatives tumble out(progenitor's embryo)in the middle of the sky.
Wood cut letters drop in lament.
Through the red soil, he rushes around the roots of trees, ignores the cavein behind, reaches at least a ground in which he can stow.
There is the sound of a train(still its vibrations through the rail)
pushing against the loose earth with his ear.
Mole!
But still he cannot hold on to this for long.

6.

Stone, unable to fall back asleep, moves into the confessional box, hoping to escape the mosquitoes, but there is spider webbing and he goes back to them. He tumbles down steps, a siren rolls through the city below. Wondering should he remain here, he hears the ocean, feels the wind pick up and the salt water ahead of him, thinking when will the day break and I can go. He lurches left and right, beginning the discension into a place he knows nothing about, hears a scream in the background of the last siren call. A lightning bug wits his face in the fragment of a mirror, reflecting a glimpse of an unshaven jowl.

He touches his face, thinks, I need to bathe.

I let him know—Sleep beneath the altar. It'll shelter until morning

A tomb a tomb a tomb he thinks.

In the burrow between the roots of a crabapple tree, he smells himself inquisitively, to find the scent of Man from his pores. With the shard of the mirror he tries to cut through exposed roots but they are

too moist. He imagines the tree scream.

He wonders is it worth it to cut the tree's root to pass through it?

but to where?

but to where?

From the altar floor, a gecko blinks once, then strikes, cracks two portions of roach, consumed full of poisonous rooms, charring its belly. He grabs his hair and apologizes for he is not sure what, sits and looks for the city(dried mouth and swollen tongued)in a clockwise spin

waiting for the sunrise

slowly enlarging

his diameter.
At his own paling(he lost the lizard's skin)moulted dead weavings
in the corners of his house.
He didn't recognize the mounting tide that came over him like a burial.
In the process of his life he tried to weave their voices and discover his tapestry. Coming tantalizingly close to food.
Unkempt and baying, nipping at one another(a deep fizzling hole)circling hoofed angels close their spiral. They gnaw at the carrion left by the card players.

Noam Mor has had short stories published in First Intensity Magazine, Prairie Winds, Downtown Brooklyn and Brooklyn Rail. "Exile," a video he produced and directed, based upon his story, "Listen Baby/I'm hot stuff/I could be/a star," was adapted into a video under a grant from The Kitchen. "Exile" was part of a video presentation at The Kitchen in December of 1996 and was part of the New York International Independent Film & Video Festival in 1997, as well as being shown at The Knitting Factory in 1998. He has had poems published in Visions International and Psychopoetica, in England. *Arc: The Cleavage of Ghosts*, is his first novel. Noam is a professor of English and philosophy in the New York City area, where he lives with his beloved.

S P U Y T E N   D U Y V I L

The Desire Notebooks

John High

ISBN 1-881471-33-0 $14.95

...accurately conveyed desire to make a novel tell the story of love and death, always and everywhere. —Publisher's Weekly

Black Lace

Barbara Henning

ISBN 1-881471-62-4 $12.00

This is Detroit circa 1970, and late one night Eileen skips out, forsaking any desire she might once have had for a regular family life. Melancholy dominates. Abandonment prevails. —Village Voice

6/2/95

Donald Breckenridge

ISBN 1-881471-77-2 $14.00

His respect for the reader's intelligence, paired with a masterful ability to convey both the isolation and unending possibilities of life in the city constitute his rare and much appreciated gift. —Mónica de la Torre

The Fairy Flag & Other Stories

Jim Savio

ISBN 1-881471-83-7 $14.00

Savio manages to create art that is profoundly political and yet unforgettable in its violence and beauty. An absolutely amazing debut collection! —Sapphire

Ted's Favorite Skirt

Lewis Warsh

ISBN 1-881471-78-0 $14.00

The heroine of *Ted's Favorite Skirt* is a hoops-shooting, Madame Bovary-reading American kid trying to figure it all out. —Laird Hunt

Little Tales of Family & War

Martha King

ISBN 1-881471-47-0 $12.00

King is a minimalist with a difference. Where much minimalist prose is dry and detached, King's is richly detailed. —American Book Review

Don't Kill Anyone, I Love You

Gojmir Polajnar

translated by Aaron Gillies

ISBN 1-881471-80-2 $12.00

Polajnar may become something of a Baltic Irvine Welsh...—Library Journal

The Poet

Basil King

ISBN 1-881471-69-1 $14.00

Spencil sketches with reminiscences of poets and writers from the early 1980's, including Baraka, Ginsberg, Berkson, Metcalf, Owen, Selby, Auster and others.

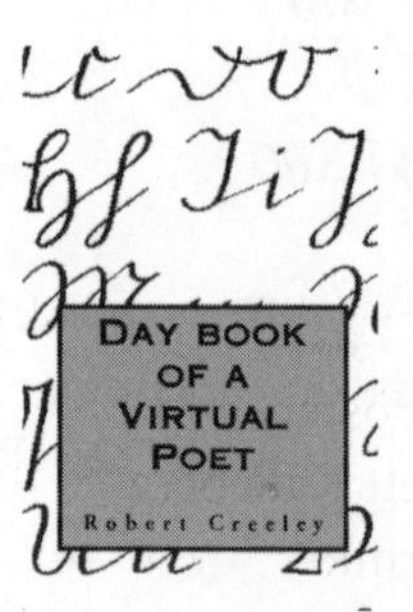

Day Book of a Virtual Poet

Robert Creeley

ISBN 1-881471-28-4 $12.00

Throughout the text, Creeley's enthusiasm never flags...—Wired Magazine

Other titles from Spuyten Duyvil

Track Norman Finkelstein
Columns (Track Volume II) Norman Finkelstein
A Flicker at the Edge of Things Leonard Schwartz
The Long & Short of It Stephen Ellis
Stubborn Grew Henry Gould
Kaleidoscope 1969 Joanna Gunderson
Identity Basil King
Warp Spasm Basil King
The Runaway Woods Stephen Sartarelli
The Open Vault Stephen Sartarelli
Cunning Laura Moriarty
Mouth of Shadows: Two Plays Charles Borkhuis
The Corybantes Tod Thilleman
Detective Sentences Barbara Henning
Are Not Our Lowing Heifers Sleeker
Than Night-Swollen Mushrooms? Nada Gordon
Gentlemen in Turbans, Ladies in Cauls John Gallaher
Spin Cycle Chris Stroffolino
Watchfulness Peter O'Leary
The Jazzer & The Loitering Lady Gordon Osing
In It What's in It David Baratier
Transitory Jane Augustine
The Flame Charts Paul Oppenheimer
Answerable to None Edward Foster
The Angelus Bell Edward Foster
Psychological Corporations Garrett Kalleberg
Moving Still Leonard Brink
See What You Think: Critical Essays
on the Next Avant Garde David Rosenberg

Spuyten Duyvil Books
are distributed to the trade by

Biblio Distribution
1-800-462-6420
WWW.BIBLIODISTRIBUTION.COM

Spuyten Duyvil
PO Box 1852
Cathedral Station
New York, New York 10025
1-800-886-5304
http://www.spuytenduyvil.net